# *The Vine II*

## *SEARCH FOR THE GOLDEN GRAIL*

ARLENE ADAMO

*The Light shines on in the
darkness,
and the darkness has never
mastered It*

*John 1:5*

# 1



"Beautifully done," Mrs. Barker chimed at her little off-key choir, as she stood in front of her junior-girls Sunday school class. She beamed with enthusiasm as she looked upon the children before her. This was her ragtag group that she would help mold into soldiers of Christ. It was a holy responsibility, and she took it very seriously.

Reaching behind her, she picked up the large white Bible and carefully opened it. Facing her class once again, she held the book firmly beneath her very prominent well-supported breasts so that each one rested securely upon an open page. She then began to tell the story she had committed to memory. This is how Mrs. Barker gave the lesson every Sunday.

Rose sat in the back of the class. She watched and listened with fascination. Mrs. Barker always told the stories as if she had been right there and seen it all. There were many stories that Rose enjoyed, and she was looking forward to hearing this one. As Mrs. Barker began to tell the tale, Rose immediately realized that today would be a disappointment. Once again, Mrs. Barker was telling the story of Lot.

Of all the stories she did not like, Rose hated this one the most. It was supposed to be a good story, but there was nothing good about it. What was wrong with Lot that he would try to protect those angels by offering his own daughters to the evil men? Mrs. Barker never mentioned what these men might do to the young women, but Rose knew they would hurt them. What was wrong with Lot? Angels didn't need protection. They were large and strong. They could do magic. His daughters were helpless, and they were his daughters. How could Lot do such an awful thing, and why would those angels let him? Mrs. Barker always told it as if Lot was some kind of hero. The entire thing made no sense, and Rose did not like it one bit. Still, there was nothing she could do but protest silently in her own mind.

As she sat on the chair swinging her legs, she suddenly forgot about Mrs. Barker and Lot. Now, she was thinking only about the slight pain in her toes and on the backs of her heels. She looked down at her shiny white plastic shoes. Her mother had bought these for the first day of school several months earlier, but now they were becoming too tight for her growing feet. Rose began to worry. What would she wear to Sunday school when these were too small? She knew that there would not be enough money to buy another fancy pair any time soon.

The Duke sat in a large wing chair and pondered the documents he had just read. Stuart had just delivered the envelope, but had no idea what it contained. He sat opposite in an identical chair and waited uncomfortably for what would come next. The Duke was visibly agitated.

"It is 1969 and I am now just hearing about this! Damned Papists! They could have shared this information before, but in their infinite divine wisdom they waited eight years after the fact! All that time, did they really believe they could uncover the mystery without my help? Arrogant fools!" he bellowed, slamming his hand into the arm of the chair.

Stuart nervously looked down and stared at the blue sapphire ring on his finger. He knew that, for now, it was best to say nothing.

The Duke got up from the chair. He began to pace, as he considered the situation. There was a great deal at stake, and he knew that he could not just share this information with anyone. He had to be careful. Walking over to the buzzer on the wall, he then pushed it to call for his servant. In less than a minute, a well-dressed servant obediently arrived at the door.

"Bring me a bottle of cognac and two glasses," the Duke grunted at the man, who quickly disappeared again. He then ran his fingers nervously through his dark grey hair and angrily plopped back down into the armchair.

Stuart thought it best to continue to remain silent; at least until the cognac arrived and the Duke had a chance to settle his nerves.

The servant soon appeared in the doorway carrying the cognac and two full snifters on a silver tray. He walked over to the Duke, bowed, and held out the offering. Without acknowledging the man, the Duke quickly grabbed the glass and greedily gulped some of it back. The servant then offered the other glass to Stuart who took it in his hand, but merely swirled the contents and sniffed.

"Leave now," the Duke commanded the servant, "and close the door on your way out." He then took another large swill from the glass.

The cognac was already beginning to work its magic, and the Duke's veins started to feel warm with renewed confidence. He took in a deep breath, looked over at Stuart and waited.

Stuart realized that the Duke expected him to say something. He tried to choose his words carefully. "Will you require my assistance, Your Grace?"

"Of course I will require your assistance, fool!" he shouted back. "You are an assistant, and so that is what you do! You assist!"

Stuart looked down at his ring again. This had been his father's ring from a time when their family name still commanded respect. He twisted it around his finger and silently waited for the Duke to continue.

The Duke took another sip of cognac and stared into his glass for a moment. He then looked back up at Stuart and in a softer tone said, "You alone, Stuart, will be privy to the information I have here. You are the only one I can trust. Your loyalty and obedience have always been unwavering."

The Duke paused and then waving the papers in the air, exclaimed, "These papers contain very important information. It is information about the Fatima visions. You, of course, know about the Fatima visions?"

"Most of what there is to know, Your Grace," replied Stuart, keeping his eyes for the most part averted, as not to risk provoking the Duke's unpredictable wrath.

"Well you do not know everything! No one knows everything about what is in the third prophecy. Even I am not privilege to that. But here, in my hand, is a piece to the puzzle. The Papists have given me this small piece in the hopes that I will help them find what it is they are looking for," said the Duke, again waving the papers in the air.

Stuart looked eagerly at the white pages in the Duke's hand. He wanted to see for himself what was written there, but the Duke did not offer them over. Instead he placed the documents back in the envelope and said, "All you need to know is why Lucia said that the third prophecy was to be opened by 1960. It was to be opened because in 1961 golden children—children, who are physically of the golden mean, would be born. Each of them would grow up to bring about change in the world. However, according to what is written, there is only one of these children whom we need to find immediately. The others are not as important. Most of them, it is said, will only make change to pave the way for her. She is the one we must find. She has the three Holy Marks which makes her more than just a golden child. It makes her the true Golden Grail. Once she reaches spiritual maturity, she will alter everything. We need to find her to ensure that she only changes what we want to be changed in this world. Certain courses must remain the same. If she belongs to us, we will own her and her power—and she does, by our divine right, belong to us."

Stuart was silent. He was quickly trying to reconcile this information with all he knew about the Duke and his superstitions. On several occasions he had attended the secret occult ceremonies, but in the role of a servant only. For him, it was just a part of his job. He assumed that the ceremonies were only the meaningless pastime of the wealthy, and privately laughed about them afterwards. He was now beginning to realize that this whole thing was bigger than he had ever imagined.

"You, handsome young Stuart," said the Duke grinning, "are going to help find this child. She could be anywhere in the world. The Bloodline is now so vast and spread out that it is difficult to know where to begin. She is not among the Papist lines. They could not find her there. She is also not among the established nobility of Europe. We have only one golden child from 1961 and she is known. Oh, you should see her, Stuart— blonde hair, blue eyes, skin as white as satin—an Aryan beauty. Not that you could appreciate female beauty, but she is a magnificent breed. She has also been set aside for our eldest son. As soon as she is of age, they shall be married. The offspring will be stupendous!"

The Duke took another long sip from his glass and then continued, "But, I am digressing. You need only concentrate on finding the missing one. I will provide you with contacts for all of the relevant groups including those in The United States, Canada and Australia. I already know from my on-going contact with the South Africans that she is not there. Wherever she is, you must find her. It is imperative that we not let that power blossom without proper guidance."

Stuart took a small sip of cognac. He was having a difficult time processing all that he was hearing. However, despite the fact that this was confusing, he recognized it as a very important moment for him personally. By being given this sensitive information along with this extremely serious task, the Duke was essentially raising Stuart's social position. He was becoming more than just a glorified butler. He was on his way to becoming the man his father wanted him to be. This was finally a chance for the status of his family branch, lost so long ago, to be restored.

There was a small knock on the door. "Enter," shouted the Duke. The servant had returned with the bottle of cognac. He walked over to the Duke bowed and held out the tray.

"No more," said the Duke, setting his empty glass on the tray and waving away the servant. He then turned back to Stuart and said, "I am feeling very confident that you can fulfill this very important mission. This is the most important task I have ever assigned to anyone, and I trust that you, of all people, will not let me down. You certainly never have before." The Duke leaned back in his chair, grinning and staring at Stuart as he stroked his chin. Stuart knew that look all too well.

The servant turned, stepped over to Stuart, bowed and held out the tray. As he placed his mostly full glass down, Stuart could not help but notice the wicked smirk on the servant's face. It was painfully obvious that this man had also recognized the way the Duke had looked over at him.

Waiting until the servant had left the room, the Duke then leaned toward Stuart and said, "Tomorrow, I will see that you receive the relevant contact information; and I expect that you will search relentlessly for the child. But for right now, you will come join me in my rooms. It has been a while since you have entertained me, young handsome Stuart."

The happy enthusiasm Stuart had felt about his new social stature was now tempered by the Duke's order. "Yes, Your Grace," he simply replied, knowing that he had no other choice. Three years ago he had been flattered by the Duke's attentions, but now, like so many other things, this had become just another wretched job to be finished and forgotten.

# 2

It was Rose's responsibility to wash the small blackboards in the five Sunday school classrooms. Her mother Jeannie, who cleaned the church every Saturday, would have preferred to do all of the work herself. She reluctantly gave Rose the blackboard work because Rose had insisted upon doing something. The task never took long, and after it was finished, Rose was expected to wait for her mother by playing quietly in a corner, or outside on the church grounds if the weather permitted.

The blackboards inside were clean, and the sun was shining as Rose sat outside at the edge of the parking lot. By lining up pebbles she had found scattered around, she was creating a picture on the asphalt in front of her. She put in the final pebble and then sat back and reflected on what she had just made. It was a simple circle with a cross right through the middle. In the center of the cross was a small piece of shiny blue-white granite. It was the prettiest pebble she had found and deserved this place of honor. Despite the varying shapes and sizes of the stones, the entire thing looked very tidy and even all the way around. She felt proud of her work, and wanted to show it to her mother.

Rose looked up at the red brick church and wondered how much longer it would take until her mother was finished. She saw Mr. Fanning come out of the side door, and walk away

13

in the other direction. He was the one who showed up that day to tell her about the church. Even though she was only six at the time, Rose remembered it well.

She had been sitting on the edge of the sidewalk, busily building a little house of sticks and grass in the hopes that it would make a good home for a ladybug, if one should wander by, when a large shadow suddenly moved over her. She looked up and there was Mr. Fanning. He wore a perfectly starched white shirt, a black suit, black tie, black hat, and shiny black shoes.

"Hello," he cheerfully sang with a big smile, "Have you heard the good news—the good news about a brand new church the good people of Texas have built just outside this lovely town of yours. They built it here just so that you might have a place to learn about glor-r-rious and wonderful things! Now please allow me to tell you about this special church. We have a super duper Sunday school there. That school is so much fun, the children are just lining up to go. A big blue bus will arrive right here at your door every Sunday morning and will take you to the school. Now, like I said before, it's not a regular school. No siree! This is a fun school where there are games, and prizes, and the good news of Jesus Christ. Wouldn't you like to be one of the lucky ones to go on the bus and get a prize every week just for showing up? All the little children are just lining up to go. But even though there is a big demand, we can always make room for one more pretty little girl like you."

At first, Rose was confused. She had never really talked with a man in a suit before. Nor had she ever seen a man with such an unwavering grin, or heard one who sang his words when he spoke. As for what he told her, it sounded like a good deal— a free bus ride, prizes and fun. She didn't know much about Jesus Christ or Texas, but the rest sounded good. Also, no one had ever called her *pretty* before. This made her feel that, just maybe, it was true.

The man could see that Rose was thinking hard about his offer. "Where's your mother?" he asked. "Is she home? Why don't you and me go and have a little talk with her? Then you can tell her just how much you would like to go to this very special and fun school.”

That was how Rose ended up at *The Light of Jesus Church*. Just weeks later, Jeannie was hired to clean the place on Saturdays, and within three months she was convinced to join the church also.

Rose was torn by her mother joining the church. The good part was that Jeannie had stopped drinking completely, but the bad part was that she now always talked too much about sin and the devil. Rose was so tired of hearing about it, but she never complained. Every day when she looked in the mirror and saw that one inch crescent shaped scar on her forehead, she was reminded about just how bad it could get when her mother was drinking. Listening to endless talk of the devil was far better than having to face him again in her mother’s eyes.

Jack sat watching the sad, but triumphant ending to the movie. There were tears in his eyes. He had seen this movie two times before and told himself that he wouldn’t cry this time, but it had happened again. He got up, turned off the television, and then sat back down, wiping away the tears. Where was Stuart? He should have been home by now. Just then he heard the sound of the key in the lock.

Stuart walked in and closed the door behind him. “I am home,” he said, without looking at Jack.

Jack had seen Stuart like this before and knew immediately where he had been. He could not just be silent. He had to say something. “Were you with him?” he asked.

“Oh Jack, I really do not want to hear it,” said Stuart, finally looking up. “You know it is not like that. I am not *with him*. I do not kiss him or hold him or speak to him of love. It is nothing at all like that. I do not even think that he is a real homo. He just….” Stuart took in a deep breath and then continued. “He just says that there are some things that men do better than women. It means nothing.”

“It means something to me, Stuart,” said Jack curtly.

"Try to understand that I do it for you."

"For me! How could any of this be for me?"

"Oh Jack, I am trying to make a better life for us. I could not possibly earn the salary I do now if I were not working for the Duke. Once we have saved enough, we will move to that place in the country. We will leave London and never look back. I promise."

"I don't want you to do this anymore, Stuart. We have enough now. We'll always get by. Please pack in this job. I can't bear thinking about you with him, and it's not just the cheating. It's because it demeans you. It's no different then the things they did to you when your father sent you away to that Public School. I just hate to see you being hurt like this."

Stuart was upset that Jack should bring up his father. What did a man like Jack know about the importance of family honor? How could he possibly understand? A sudden rage welled up within him, and he felt like he wanted to break something. "And what if a man as important and noble as the Duke requests my exquisite talents for pleasure!" he yelled. "We are homos, aren't we? Isn't that the kind of thing we do? Fornicate like dogs—anywhere and anytime! We are animals— just animals! And this animal plans to get as much as he can! It is the law of the jungle for dogs like us!"

"Oh please no," pleaded Jack, "don't talk like that. You know it isn't true. We are men, Stuart, not dogs! Don't say such horrible things! All that I want in this life is to live with you in peace and with dignity. I want us to be happy. That is all."

Stuart could not stay in that room any longer. He walked down the hall to the bathroom and locked the door behind him. Turning on the shower, he then quickly stripped off all of his clothes and stepped in. The warm water washed over him, and he tried as best he could to try and feel clean. He now felt sick about how he had yelled at Jack. It shouldn't have happened. Leaning his head against the cold, hard tiles, he imagined smashing his skull against them again and again. "Oh God, oh God, oh God," he sobbed. His tears mixed with the water that streamed down his face, but it was not enough to wash away his pain.

# 3

It had been weeks since the Duke gave Stuart the task of finding the child, and so far he had found nothing. He had traveled to several places in Europe without finding as much as a clue. Once, he was approached by some worshipers of Odin who told him that they had heard he was looking for a golden child, and that they knew where she was. They claimed that she was behind the Communist controlled borders of Latvia, but when Stuart saw the photos, he could immediately tell that she was not even close to being golden. The Odin worshipers were not happy about his conclusions, and he barely escaped with his life.

Stuart sat at his desk and looked at the piles of useless papers in front of him. After all of the work—all of those phone calls and meetings—all of it had come to nothing. If he failed at this task, could there ever be any hope of restoring his family status? The Duke would never forgive him if he failed.

As he looked discouragingly at the mess in front of him, he could not help but notice the crystal unicorn sitting on the corner of the desk. For a moment, the gloom lifted and he smiled. This had been a running joke between him and Jack. When they first met, Jack had only just arrived from Liverpool and had absolutely no taste. One of the first presents he ever gave Stuart was a hideous over-sized porcelain unicorn. Stuart pretended to love it, but once Jack became more educated in London culture, he recognized his mistake and began to purposefully purchase the silliest unicorns he could find. Not a birthday or holiday went by without Stuart receiving some form of this ridiculous mythical creature. He chose this one to bring to the office because it was the least gaudy and would not be easily noticed.

Suddenly, the door flew open and the Duke marched in. Stuart immediately stood up like a soldier at attention.

"Well, you have been busy," said the Duke, surveying the piles of papers on the desk. "However, I understand that, as of yet, you have found nothing. Is this correct?"

"Yes, Your Grace. There have been no real leads of any kind," replied Stuart. He wanted to explain just how hard he had been working, and how difficult it was, but he knew all too well that excuses were never acceptable.

"You disappoint me Stuart," said the Duke, who with a swipe of his arm pushed a pile of papers onto the floor. The crystal unicorn almost fell to the floor too, but Stuart caught it just in time.

The Duke laughed and sat on the edge of the cleared desk. He gestured for Stuart to sit in the chair. Stuart quickly obeyed and then looked up at the Duke. "Do not despair," the Duke said. "I have something you will very much like." He paused and just grinned for what seemed like the longest time.

Stuart sat awkwardly waiting, until finally, the Duke began to speak again. "I believe that I have found a man who may just hold the secret. I have reason to suspect that he possesses information that will help lead us to our little golden rose. Unfortunately, this man will not talk to me Stuart. It is a very long story, but I am afraid that he just does not like me at all. You, however, are the key. We can get him to talk to you. I am certain of it."

"And why would he talk to me, Your Grace?" asked Stuart.

The Duke leaned in closer and said, "Because you are family, and I believe that he will talk to family. He is your uncle—your dear old uncle Marlon."

Although he had never actually met the man before, Stuart knew that he had an uncle. His father had, on occasion, talked about him. Stuart understood that Marlon was the son of his grandfather's first wife, and only a half-brother to his father. Marlon was much older than his father. He was already a young man and had left home by the time his father was born. At some point, Marlon had committed a horribly traitorous act and was banished from the family. Stuart knew that his father never forgave his brother and hated him right to the end.

"How could it be that my Uncle Marlon would know how to find her? He was turned out from the family long ago," said Stuart. "My father said that he had shamed them by secretly marrying an outsider. After that, he had no more contact with anyone on the inside. Where would his information come from?"

"Well, all that is true. However, he is still part of the Underground," said the Duke. "You have not been told about this before, but there is an Underground where traitors like your uncle undermine our accomplishments. They do not believe in divine right, and do things contrary to our path as God's chosen.

Stuart was shocked. He had always been taught that if you were not with the family than you were essentially dead, and no longer privy to any family secrets. You were no longer of The Great Work and would become just part of the ordinary rabble. The idea that there could be a family group working independently, and even working covertly, seemed amazing to him. "How long has there been an Underground, Your Grace?" he asked.

"For a very long time," replied the Duke. "We try to encourage them back into the fold, whenever we can. If that does not work, we assess the threat and do what is necessary. Your uncle has been a difficult hold-out. Over the years, there has been nothing I have offered that has enticed him to return. We were actually in the process of assessing him when we learned that he may have the knowledge we require."

"And why do you believe that I can get my uncle to talk, Your Grace? I have never even met the man."

The Duke tapped his fingers on the desk and grinned. "Because you, sweet Stuart, are the nearest blood kin he has left in this world. He never had any children of his own, and his wife is dead. I know that you will be able to ingratiate yourself with him. You must gain his complete trust. It should not be too difficult. Marlon is just the kind of sentimental old fool who would be elated to have his long lost nephew show up on his doorstep. All you have to do is be your natural charming self, and make him feel that he can depend on you. This will allow you to get close enough to find the information he is hiding. Do this successfully Stuart, and you will receive a thirty thousand pound bonus."

Stuart was not sure if he heard correctly. "Thirty thousand?" he asked in disbelief.

"Yes," replied the Duke, "all that money plus—I shall ensure that you receive a fitting title."

Stuart could not believe his ears. A title—a title meant everything to him. It meant much more than the money. Such a thing would definitely restore the honor of his family branch. Finally, everything that went wrong, would be put right again.

"Oh yes, Your Grace! Of course, I will do whatever you require of me."

"I knew that I could rely on your loyalty," smiled the Duke. "Have my secretary provide you with the directions to Marlon's home. He resides in the country, but not far from London. Acquiring his complete trust could take a little time, so I suggest you get out there as soon as possible."

The Duke slid off of the desk and headed for the door. Just before he left, he turned and said, "Oh by the way, I will be holding another party this Friday evening, and you will be escorting Lady Alexa Spence. She requires a date and her parents asked if I would find someone respectable within the Bloodline—preferably someone who would not threaten her virtue." The Duke laughed loudly and went out the door.

Stuart got down on his knees and began to pick up the scattered papers on the floor. *A title and thirty thousand pounds*, he kept thinking to himself. Not only would he be able to buy a lovely country property for himself and Jack, but he would also fulfill his father's final wish. He looked at the sapphire ring that sparkled on his finger. A wonderful day was certainly drawing near.

* * *

Rose looked at the big white paper in front of her. The teacher had instructed the class to "draw a lovely spring day." Rose glanced across at the pictures being drawn by the children in the next row. Every one of them started with a big yellow sun in the right hand corner.  She did not want to draw a big sun. She was not sure what she wanted to draw.

Rose looked at the small box of crayons on her desk. There were only eight different colors to choose from. Why were there not more colors? She wanted there to be more colors, but knew that eventually she would have to pick from one of the eight. The other children were furiously coloring their green grasses and blue skies, and she still had a blank page.

Finally, Rose picked up the red crayon and made a long waving line right in the middle of her paper. She looked at the line and wondered. Then she drew a curved line that met the waving line at each end. Now she had a strange shape that looked almost like a fish. In the widest part of the shape she drew a circle, and then another circle inside of that. She colored in the inner circle, and finished the whole thing off with a third waving line above. Rose stopped and stared at what she had done. It was an eye—a big, long, waving red eye!

As she sat staring, one of the other children noticed what she had done. "Look!" the girl said. "Look what Rose did!"

All of the children turned to look at Rose's page. "What is that?" one of them exclaimed.

"It's a crazy *Injun* thing," said Glen, who took the opportunity to call Rose an *Injun* whenever he could.

"I'm telling," said one of the girls. "Mrs. Simpson!" she called, putting her hand up. "Rose has drawed an Indian eye."

Mrs. Simpson walked back to Rose's desk and looked at her paper. "Rose, what is this?" she asked.

21

Rose had her head down. She wanted to cry with everyone staring at her, but with everyone staring at her, she knew that she had better not.

"It's an *Injun* eye," said Glen, and all the children laughed.

"Glen the correct word is Indian," said Mrs. Simpson, sternly. She then said to Rose, "You cannot just draw whatever you like. You must follow instructions, and you knew that you were to draw a spring day." Mrs. Simpson picked up Rose's paper. "Well, we should not be wasting good paper so let us just turn it over and you may draw your picture on the other side. If you need ideas, then look around at some of the other drawings. The rest of the class is doing such fine work."

Mrs. Simpson walked back to the front of the room, and Glen whispered over to Rose, "Weirdo *Injun*."

For a moment, Rose just sat looking at her paper. She then reached over and picked up a yellow crayon. In the right-hand corner of the page, she drew a circle for the sun. She continued to draw a picture as per Mrs. Simpson's instructions—a picture similar to what the other children were drawing. As she colored in the green grass at the bottom, she could not help but notice the red showing through from the other side. She tried to concentrate only on the picture she was drawing, but there it was—that great red eye staring right through and straight at her.

# 4

It was drizzling rain as Stuart drove along the old country road. He had passed through the small town of Stalbridge and, according to the directions he was given, knew that he should be coming upon the lane soon. At some point he suspected he must have missed it, and so he turned the car around to check again.  His instincts were right, and he soon spotted the old dirt lane that was almost hidden by heavy vegetation on both sides. He turned the wheel and headed down the long winding path.

Eventually, a charming fieldstone cottage came into view. It was very traditional with an old sloping thatched roof and plenty of windows. There was smoke coming from the large chimney.

Stuart stopped the car and pulled up the hood of his raincoat. He opened the door, and went to step out. As soon as his foot hit the ground, his shoe slid uncontrollably and he fell hard. It turned out that not only was the ground quite soft where he had parked, but there was also a small incline. The result was that he now found himself sitting in mud.

Slowly, so as not to lose his footing again, Stuart pulled himself up using the car door handle. He then carefully made his way around the car to firmer ground. It was only then that he realized that his raincoat must have slid up when he fell, providing no protection for his clothes. He could now feel the cold wet mud soaking straight through his pants. Stuart wondered if he should simply turn around and go home.

Just as he was seriously considering getting back in the car and driving away, a voice shouted, "You should have parked closer to the house!"

Stuart looked over and saw an old man in the doorway of the cottage. The man beckoned to him, "Don't just stand there in the rain. Come in, come in."

Still a little nervous about the solidity of the ground beneath his feet, Stuart made his way to the cottage door. "Come in," said the old man, moving aside to make way for Stuart. "Watch your head. Our ancestors were short people and built their homes accordingly."

Stuart stood just inside the open door, dripping mud and water on the rug. He could now get a good look at the man who had welcomed him inside the cottage. Although this man appeared to be quite old, he still possessed a handsome look of health and strength. He still looked full of life.

The man closed and latched the door. "I am very glad you are here, Stuart," he said with a smile.

Stuart was shocked, and his heart began to beat faster. The old man knew his name! How did he know who he was? Did he know why he was there? How powerful was this Underground? Should he now try to escape with his life?

The man laughed when he saw the look of alarm on Stuart's face. "Oh, not to worry. I am not a mind reader—not an ESP expert. You happen to look much like my brother did at your age. That is how I know who you are."

Stuart smiled and with some embarrassment said, "Oh I am so sorry. Where are my manners? I must have left them out in the rain. You are, of course, my Uncle Marlon, and I am your nephew—your nephew Stuart."

The old man held out his hand and laughingly said, "Well, now that we are both certain as to who we are, I am very pleased to meet you nephew."

When Stuart shook his uncle's warm dry hand, he suddenly became aware that his own hand was very cold and damp. He did not know why, but it made him feel a little ashamed.

Marlon looked Stuart up and down. "You are a mess," he said.

Stuart laughed. "I suppose I am," he responded, looking down at his expensive clothing and shoes covered in mud.

"Well my clothes won't do. I'm wider than you, and you are taller than I. Still, I should be able to find something for you to wear whilst your things dry. Take off your shoes and I will see what I have."

Marlon left the room, and Stuart crouched down to remove his shoes. While he did, he had a good look around. The room had a low beamed ceiling and was full of antique English furniture. A large stone fireplace designed for cooking dominated the far end, and an old iron kettle hung above the burning fire.

When his uncle returned, Stuart had already removed his shoes and put his coat on a nearby hook. Marlon was holding what appeared to be some blue striped pajamas. He held them out to Stuart and said, "Now these are completely new—never worn. They were a Christmas present to me from the widow down the road, but they are too big. I suppose that I am a much bigger man in her mind. She's after me, you know. Although I suspect that what she really wants is a lap dog, not a husband." Stuart laughed with his uncle and accepted the pajamas.

"There is a little room through there," said Marlon, pointing at a plain wooden door. "You may use that to change."

Stuart entered the room, and closed the door behind him. It seemed to be a small library with bookshelves on every wall. There was a single comfortable chair and reading lamp in the corner. He set down the pajamas on the chair and quickly began to take off his clothes. It suddenly became clear that the water had soaked through everything, including his shirt tail. Once he had stripped down to his underwear, he pondered what to do next. The back of his white briefs were completely saturated with water and mud. This was a real problem. He couldn't just simply hand over his underwear to a man he had just met, even if that man were his uncle. But if he put on the pajamas over the wet underwear, the water and mud could soak through, and that would be worse. For a moment, he just stood there and thought.

Finally, he stripped off the underwear and took the only option he could see available. He kicked them far back under the chair.

Stuart opened the door and walked out wearing the blue striped pajamas. In his hand, he carried all of his wet things. He was feeling more than a little embarrassed about the entire situation.

Marlon was sitting on a stool near the fire cleaning the mud off Stuart's shoes. There was a second stool and a small table with a porcelain tea set nearby. "Come and sit down here," said Marlon, pointing to the empty stool. "That rain can chill your very bones."

Stuart walked over and sat down. Marlon took Stuart's clothes from him and hung them to dry near the fireplace. He then sat back down and began to work on the shoe again.

"Uncle, you do not have to clean my shoes."

"Oh it is no problem," replied Marlon. "I am almost done. If you let the mud dry on expensive shoes like these, they will be ruined completely. They are designed for prestige, not durability. There you see, all finished." Marlon set the shoe down beside the other one that he had cleaned while Stuart was busy changing.

"You are very kind," said Stuart, "especially when I have arrived without giving you any notice at all.

"Oh I don't mind. It is just good to finally meet you, and to finally find someone to fit those pajamas." Marlon laughed and Stuart smiled.

"I believe the tea is ready," said Marlon, pouring out two cups. "You, my son, have never had tea like this. I heat the water over an open fire in that old iron kettle you see there. That is the secret. Even the most inexpensive tea bag can create the nectar of the gods if the water is right. Milk? Sugar?"

"Only milk please," replied Stuart.

"Just like your uncle," said Marlon handing him the cup. "I could never tolerate sugar in my tea either."

Stuart brought the cup to his lips and sipped the hot brew. He could feel it move down through his chest and into his stomach. It began to warm him through, driving the cold from his veins. "Why Uncle, this really is exceptional tea! Certainly, the best I have ever tasted."

Marlon smiled and simply responded, "Yes, it is."

"Uncle, I have wished to meet you for a very long time now." Stuart felt uncomfortable having to lie to the nice old man, but he reminded himself that he had a mission to accomplish. Everything he had ever really wanted in life was now at stake. "Since I was a boy and heard my father mention you, I have thought that I must one day find you."

After taking a sip of tea, Marlon smiled and said, "Well, I am very glad you have found me."

"Father never said why you and he were no longer in contact. He only said that he did not want to talk about it. Whatever occurred between you two, I think, was a terrible thorn he endured his entire life. Actually, his last words to me were about you." Stuart could not look at his uncle, and continued to just look from the fireplace to his teacup and back again. "Would you like to know what he said, Uncle Marlon?"

"Certainly I would," replied Marlon still smiling.

"Well, as he lay there dying, he said to me, 'Stuart, I have only one regret in my life. I regret that I never made peace with my brother. If you ever get the chance dear son, please promise me you will try to make this right. I only wish that I had time to remedy this myself, but my time is at an end.' Within mere moments my dear father passed away." Stuart kept his head down and tried as best he could to look sad.

"My word," exclaimed Marlon scratching his chin, "that is quite a surprise—my brother, at the very end, wanting to make peace with me. And now here you are, so that I might learn of his final wishes. Why, it's like a happy movie ending, isn't it?"

Stuart looked up and smiled at the old man. "Why yes Uncle, I suppose it is like a happy movie. I hope now that we have met, we may continue to get to know each other better. It is peculiar, but it seems as if my father has come back through me, and somehow I will be able to create his peace with you. I will be able to fulfill his final wish."

"That is certainly a lovely thought, Stuart," replied Marlon. "And in the spirit of lovely thoughts, why don't you go back to London—I suppose that you still live in London—pack a bag and then return. You may stay with me for a week or even two—that is, if it does not interfere with work or anything else. I believe the fresh country air will do you a great deal of good, and we may then properly get to know each other."

Stuart was stunned. This was easier than he ever imagined. The old man was just as gullible and sentimental as the Duke had described him. "Oh Uncle," replied Stuart, "that is a wonderful idea! It should not be a problem to get time off work, and I am well over-due for a vacation in the country."

"I am certain that you are," said Marlon, as he topped up their cups of tea. "Your clothes are almost dry, but you must have more tea before you go."

"Thank you Uncle. I believe I will." Stuart sipped back some more of the hot tea and thought about whether he would become an Earl, or should he not raise his hopes too much and only expect to be a Baron.

* * *

Jack was working in the kitchen when Stuart arrived home. Stuart was actually the better cook, but because of his unpredictable hours, Jack often found himself doing the cooking. He resented this a little because Stuart could be fussy about food, and was not always as appreciative as he should be.

Stuart came into the kitchen and placed his hand on Jack's shoulder. "What are you making?" he asked.

"Nothing special, just some salmon fillets, but I hope you like it," replied Jack.

"I am sure I will." Stuart turned and as he was walking out added, "I just need to change my clothes."

When Stuart returned wearing a fresh pair of slacks and a clean shirt, Jack was no longer in the kitchen and had left the fish frying at too high a temperature. Stuart took the pan from the hot element and turned it off. He then went to the living room to search for Jack.

Jack was sitting on the sofa. He was visibly upset. In his hand was an open brown paper bag. "Would you like to explain?" he asked Stuart, expecting the worst.

Stuart could see that Jack was holding the paper bag with the pajamas his uncle had given him. He couldn't help himself and began to laugh.

"How could you be so cruel!" shouted Jack.

"No Jack, it's not what you think."

"It's never *that,* is it Stuart?"

"You have to believe me. They were a present from my uncle."

"What uncle?" asked Jack, who had never heard Stuart mention an uncle before.

"He is my long lost uncle. I have only just recently found out where he is living, and that is where I was today. I was meeting my Uncle Marlon for the very first time. He's quite old, so there was no putting it off. I wanted to be sure I had a chance to meet him. His wife is dead and he has no children. I am his last remaining relation. To be honest, I just showed up unannounced, but he was quite gracious to me anyway."

Jack was still a little unsure. Stuart had lied before, but he was very bad at it. Either he had suddenly gotten better, or he was telling the truth.

"Now that we are on the subject, I also should tell you that I will be staying a few days with him. He invited me so that we might have a chance to get to know each other better. It is a very quaint old cottage in the country. You would love it, Jack."

"And did you happen to tell this uncle about me?" asked Jack, still wondering if this was the real story.

Stuart laughed nervously. "I just met him today. I think it might be a little much if I told the man, 'by the way, I am a homo and may I tell you all about my companion.' Give it some time, and when and if it seems okay, I shall broach the subject."

Jack looked again at the pajamas in the bag. They certainly did look like something an old man would pick out. He decided that Stuart was telling the truth, at least for the most part. "I'm sorry Stuart. I just thought the worst."

"You don't have to be sorry Jack. It's not as if I haven't given you good reason not to trust me. I promise that from now on I will be completely honest with you." Stuart felt that not telling him about the Duke's mission did not officially count as a lie. There were some things Jack should not know.

"And just to ensure that you know everything, I shall be back temporarily on Friday, but only to escort Lady Alexa Spence to the Duke's party"

"You wouldn't actually do anything with her, would you?" asked Jack, who was now feeling a renewed sense of distrust. Lately, it was becoming more and more difficult to be sure just where he stood with Stuart.

"I will do what my job requires. I will charm her. I will dance with her. I will hold her hand. And at the end of the night I will probably feign an advance which will flatter her, but which will also cause her to severely rebuff me. It is only theatre, Jack."

"You know that I would never stand for it if you married one of these girls. I would never wait on the side, in hopes that you could find an excuse and sneak away. I could not live like that. I could never live a life that was *but a walking shadow*." Jack would often quote Shakespeare whenever emotions were high, and he wanted to be sure that he was heard.

"Jack, I am not marrying any girl. You are my life and I will not leave you—ever."

Jack smiled slightly and said, "Just promise me that when you visit your uncle, you'll consider telling him about me. It would be nice to be a part of your life outside of this flat."

"He seems like a kind man, and as soon as the time is right, I promise I will tell him."

"Thank you Stuart. So much of our life is about lying and hiding away. It would be a pleasant change to have someone we could be completely honest with. I hope your uncle is that sort of man. I hate having to hide the truth."

"We had better finish cooking our meal if it is at all still salvageable," said Stuart, wanting to change the subject.

Jack was certain there was something more that Stuart was not telling him, but decided now was not the time to ask questions. He knew that Stuart was under a lot of pressure lately and was worried about him. Perhaps a visit with this newly found uncle might be just the thing he needed.

# 5

Rose lay on her back in the grass looking up at the clouds. She remembered a time when she thought heaven was in the sky. That's what the pictures from her Sunday school handouts told her. Sometimes she would just wait and watch to see if an angel would peek over the edge. It was only after she noticed how the airplanes flew straight through the clouds that she realized there was no heaven there at all.

That's not the only lie they told at the Sunday school. They also taught her that when people were mean or bad, God made their hearts turn black. They even showed pictures of it. Rose believed them and tried not to be bad so that her heart would not shrivel up and kill her. It was only in a conversation with her neighbor Lizzy that she realized this was not true.

Lizzy was two years older than Rose. Her father wore a suit to work, and her mother went to the beauty parlor once a week. There had been times when Lizzy invited Rose over to play in her yard, and Rose went because it always seemed like a good idea at the time. Now Rose tried to avoid Lizzy as much a possible. She knew that even if Lizzy smiled and acted friendly, eventually the fun would come to an abrupt end with her saying something cruel. That is exactly how it went on the day Rose found out the truth about black hearts.

"I can only play outside with you 'cause my mother says you're not allowed in my house. She says it's 'cause you're dirty and you smell," said Lizzy, in the nonchalant and sudden way she usually said these types of things.

"You're mean," said Rose. "Your heart is turning black and you will die."

Lizzy laughed. "My heart isn't turning black."

"It is too," said Rose, almost crying. "I learned it at my Sunday school. When you're mean your heart will turn black and you die." At that point, she could almost see Lizzy's heart shriveling up.

"You're an idiot. Your heart doesn't really turn black. Those crazy people at your church are just making it all up."

When Lizzy said those words, it suddenly all became clear. No matter how much she wanted to, Rose could not deny it. Lizzy was right. Her heart was not turning black. She was sitting there just as alive as ever. Being cruel would not make her heart stop beating. Those church people had not told her the truth, and made her look stupid in front of Lizzy. They lied when they made her believe that the world was fair and orderly. It was nothing like that, and Lizzy herself was proof of this.

Rose felt a little angry remembering that day. She pulled up a handful of grass from beside her and let it rain down on her stomach. When people lied so much, it was not always easy to tell what was what. Even though the church people didn't know what they were talking about, she still loved God and she still loved Jesus. They were real. Rose knew this for certain. Like her, people sometimes said things about Them that were just not true; and like her, They too had to navigate around so many things that were wrong in the world.

* * *

The morning was warm and the sun was shining when Stuart arrived at his uncle's cottage. Because the ground remained a little soft from the rain the day before, he was careful to follow Marlon's advice and park closer to the house. As he was taking his suitcase out of the trunk, Marlon came out and greeted him. "Well, this is certainly a more pleasant day," he happily exclaimed.

"Good day Uncle Marlon. Yes, it is most definitely an improvement."

"Come in then, and I'll show you to your room."

Stuart followed his uncle into the cottage and up the narrow stairs. They entered the first room on the left.

"This is it," said Marlon. "I hope you do not mind the yellow rose wallpaper, or the Da Vinci prints. This was your Aunt Lily's quiet room, where she could go and shut the door whenever she wished to be alone for a while. After she passed on, I was able to change it into a spare bedroom, but could not bring myself to change the walls in any way."

Stuart quickly looked around the very bright and feminine room with its two south facing dormer windows. "It is a lovely room and I am sure I will be very comfortable here," he said politely.

"Well, the kettle is on, and how do you fancy a proper English breakfast? That is, if you are hungry?"

Stuart had only tea and a slice of toast before leaving London. He suddenly realized that his stomach was indeed feeling quite empty. "That sounds wonderful! Thank you Uncle."

"Very well then, while I go prepare a grand fry-up, you take your time and get settled. I want you to feel at home here." Marlon patted Stuart on the shoulder and left.

Now that he was alone, Stuart took a good look around the room. Everything about it made him feel uneasy, but he didn't know why. Taking a closer look at the seven prints on the four walls he realized that they were all of women. He was completely surrounded by Da Vinci's women! His discomfort deepened even more.

Stuart tried his best not to look at them, but Mona Lisa would not stop staring at him, and as for Leda—well that was even worse. Finally, he forced his eyes down, placed his suitcase on the bed, and began to unpack.

As he placed his things in the dresser drawers, he tried to think about the kinds of things he could say to make the old man trust him. He tried as best he could to keep focused on developing a sure-fire strategy. However, his focus kept slipping. Try as he may, he just could not concentrate. Every time he almost had his train of thought, his eyes would always be drawn back towards Mona Lisa. He knew that he had to resist her, but her smile kept knocking all of the thoughts straight out of his head.

*  *  *

It had been raining for the past three days, but today the sun was shining warm and bright. Rose was so happy to finally get a chance to go outside and play. She was tired of being stuck inside for so long.

When she opened the door she saw, to her delight, a large puddle in her dirt driveway. Quickly, she kicked off her shoes and ran over to it. At first, she dipped in only her toes. It was fresh and cool. Slowly, she walked in until the water was up to her calves. The mud on the bottom was soft and squishy under her feet. Rose began to walk around and around the puddle, making up a song from something she had heard in Sunday school.

*Oh little children keep yourselves from idols*
*Oh little children keep yourselves from idols*
*Oh little children keep yourselves from idols*
*Or the dark black mud will swallow you whole.*

Something in the air suddenly caught Rose's eye, and she stopped singing. It was a Monarch butterfly. "Hello beautiful butterfly," said Rose. "You're very early." The butterfly landed at the edge of the puddle.

Rose watched as it took a drink of water, then opened its wings wide and flew upwards. She tried to keep her eye on where it was going, but it had disappeared.

Still standing in the middle of the puddle, Rose only wished that the butterfly would return. She closed her eyes and prayed, "God, please bring back my butterfly." When she opened her eyes, she could see nothing in the air in front of her. Rose felt defeated. She knew it was not always right to ask God for things, but thought that maybe this was important enough to be an exception.

Ready to turn and go back inside, Rose then looked down. What she saw filled her with joy! Their majestic colorful wings were gently opening and closing like banners of victory. There on the front of her shirt, five great Monarchs nobly rested.

* * *

As Stuart came downstairs, he could smell warm delicious food. It was only then that he realized just how hungry he truly was. He walked into the kitchen and saw his uncle busily preparing their meal.

"All settled?" asked Marlon, while turning the sausages in the pan.

"Yes, thank you," replied Stuart. "It is a very comfortable room."

"Food will be ready shortly. The tea is already brewed. Sit down at the table, pour a cuppa and tell me all about yourself." Marlon shook some salt on the frying eggs.

Stuart sat down and poured some tea. "Let's see—where should I begin? Well really, there is not much to tell. I work for an advertising agency. It is a good job and a decent salary."

"Oh really," said Marlon, "I know most of the advertising agencies in London. Which one do you work for?"

Stuart shifted a little in his chair, and twisted his ring. "I do not believe you would know this company. It is rather new and still quite small."

"You never know. What's it called?"

Stuart hesitated for a moment. All he could think about while under this pressure was Mona Lisa smiling at him. "It is called Mano Lasi Advertising," he said.

"Mano Lasi," said Marlon. "Well, that is an interesting name."

"That is the name of the company owner," said Stuart, thinking quickly. "He's a… uh…foreigner. His name is Mano Lasi."

"And do you like working for Mr. Lasi?" asked Marlon.

"Oh yes," exclaimed Stuart, "he is a very fair employer."

Marlon brought two full plates over to the table, set one in front of Stuart and then sat down opposite.

"Well go ahead, try it," said Marlon.

Stuart took some egg on his fork and placed it in his mouth. "Mmmm. That is very good uncle," he said, glad that he could at least be honest about that.

"I am happy you like it," said Marlon, pouring himself a cup of tea. "So tell me more about yourself."

"I am as yet a bachelor, but I must confess that there is someone special in my life," Stuart said, taking another bite.

"And who is this someone?" asked Marlon.

"Well, I was going to tell you anyway because I must leave on Friday to meet her. You see, I promised to escort her to a party that evening. I can return on Saturday, if that is alright with you, but my Friday night has already been promised to her. Her name is Lady Alexa Spence. Perhaps you have heard of her?"

Marlon looked at Stuart. "Yes," he replied, "or rather, I should say that I know her family. And so—this girl—you think she might be the one?"

"She is certainly a lovely and virtuous girl Uncle, and from the Bloodline. I have a good feeling that she just may be the one." Stuart looked at Marlon and smiled confidently.

Marlon looked at Stuart, sighed and then began to eat again. In between bites, he said, "As your Aunt Lily used to say, *Eat up man, afore the devil knows you're hungry.*"

# 6

Rose was sitting on a branch about eight feet from the ground. She loved to climb this old tree on the hill. From here, she could see a long way. The tree was older than the farmer's fence and the gravel road that were on either side of it. Because it was in this middle place, no man had ever got it in his mind to cut it down or even trim it. It grew naturally, with large lower branches that made it perfect for climbing.

Rose rested her head against the tree trunk and looked out at all she could see. The houses in the distance looked very peaceful and quiet. It seemed as though everyone had gone to sleep. She closed her eyes and thought about the story of Sleeping Beauty. Perhaps the whole world really was asleep, and while they all slept, the vines were growing over everything. In her mind, she could see the vines wrapping up the trees and houses, blocking roads and doorways. What would the people do when they awakened only to find out what had happened to their world?

There was a sudden noise below and Rose opened her eyes. She saw Lizzy's dog Runy chasing a rabbit into the bushes. Rose hated Runy. His coat was burnished red and his nose was pointed. He looked more like a very large fox than like a dog. Runy did not have big warm brown eyes like other dogs. His were black and empty, and his bone-thin tail never wagged.

Rose didn't want to think about Runy anymore, so she turned her face towards the sky. The sight of soft white clouds resting in the sea of blue brought her comfort. Despite everything, the world was still a good place to be. She watched with fascination as several birds flew by. If only she could fly too. Staring into the endless sky, she tried to imagine what it would be like to soar freely through the air. Just to leap forward and be taken on the wind. No walls, no ground to stumble over, nothing in your way—only eternity. As she thought about flying, Rose began to feel as light as the air. It seemed as though her entire body were slowly melting into the sky, and she could sense that she was about to float away. All of a sudden, a fear of falling came over her and jolted her back to the solid world.

Rose sighed and rested her head against the tree trunk once again. As she looked out in the direction of her house, she suddenly became aware of the growing hunger in her stomach. It was getting close to suppertime. She placed her feet on the next branch and began to climb down.

When Rose reached the lowest branch, she jumped to the ground and immediately took off running. Halfway down the hill, she could feel that her shoelace was undone. In one sudden motion, she stopped and crouched down to tie it. The second she did, something large whizzed straight over her head. She looked up just in time to see Runy sliding painfully along the gravel road. Without looking back, he immediately jumped up and ran off into the woods. Rose knew that the dog was running in fear by what had just happened. She also knew that he would not try that again.

Stuart sat in the garden chair and looked out at the beautiful countryside view. *Jack would love this*, he thought to himself. So far the visit with his uncle was going very well, but he needed to turn their casual conversations towards more serious matters. He needed to get closer to learning the information his uncle had.

Marlon came out with a tea tray in hand. "You seem to bring good luck," he smiled. That is now two days in a row that the sun is shining."

He set down the tray on a small table and began pouring the tea. Marlon handed a cup to Stuart.

"Thank you uncle, and thank you so much again for having me. This is such a wonderful break from cold grey London."

"So you do not love the city, like your father did?" asked Marlon.

Stuart was glad he had mentioned his father. This would help him steer the conversation where he wanted it to go. "He certainly did love London, and I suppose I am very fond of it also. However, the country has its advantages." Stuart paused and then sipped his tea. "Yes," he continued, "my dear Father died in the city that he loved. But today, I am so happy that I am now here to fulfill his dying wish. He wanted you to know that he deeply regretted your banishment, and wished only that you would return to the family."

"Well, that is a surprise," said Marlon.

"I assure you that it was very heartfelt, and he did weep, Uncle. It was the first time I had ever seen my father cry before." Stuart lowered his head partly for the dramatic effect, but also because he could not look Marlon in the eye.

"And do you believe that I should return to the family?" asked Marlon.

"Oh Uncle, nothing would make me happier than if you came back to be a recognized part of the Bloodline once again."

"And why would I consider doing that?" said Marlon. "The Bloodline is nothing but a big bloody mess!" he shouted, slamming his hand down on the arm of the chair.

Stuart was taken aback. This quiet harmless old man was suddenly roaring like a lion. And to say what he did about the family? Stuart had never heard anyone talk like that before. Being a part of the family was the mark of greatness and a source of pride.

Marlon saw the look on Stuart's face and sighed. "I know that my reaction surprises you, but think about it my son. Almost two thousand years of human reproduction has resulted in millions of these descendants walking around with many of them suffering from an over-inflated sense of entitlement and self-importance. That is what the Bloodline really is. We are not God's special children. There is no magic in our blood that is not in the blood of every human being on this earth."

Stuart sat in silence. He hadn't expected this at all, and did not know what to say.

"And what are the Holy Marks, Stuart? What does any of it really mean? Throughout history there have been those who have possessed a Holy Mark, but who have done the most unholy things imaginable. So much of it is just a big bloody lie!"

"But Uncle," said Stuart, "we are the children of our Lord Father Jesus Christ. How can you say that there is nothing special about us? Do you say that there was nothing special about Him?"

"No Stuart, that is not what I am saying," said Marlon, tracing his finger along the chair arm. "Everything was special about our Holy Father, but where did He come from? Not from a Zeus man-god with a fetish for virgins as the Romans made the people believe. You and I both know better. He came from the flesh and blood of an ordinary man and an ordinary woman. That is what makes His story so wonderful and that is what truly gives us all hope."

Stuart stayed silent and tried to take in all his uncle was saying. It was, of course, common knowledge within the Bloodline that the Romans lied, but it was always accepted that keeping up the lie helped the Bloodline to thrive.

"Our Father came from the people. He belonged to the ordinary people. The Romans stole Him away. They took Him, stripped Him of His humanity, turned His blood to molten iron and made Him into an idol. Then they used Him to enslave the very people He loved the most."

Stuart was still speechless. He looked out at the distant barley field, and tried to gather his thoughts.

"So many in the Bloodline are completely misguided," Marlon continued. "And you may not want to hear it, but your father was among them. He was so angry at me. To him, I threw away everything by marrying a common Irish woman. I shamed the family and ruined his opportunities. He took it very personally and never forgave me for that. He thought that I should marry within the Bloodline—that I should be bred out like a kennel dog!"

Stuart saw an opening and exclaimed, "But he changed Uncle—in the end he saw how important you were to him and he forgave you."

Marlon completely ignored this and said, "Your father believed in the idea that the blood must be kept pure—as if there were such a thing. He once wrote me a letter to tell me that he was happy to learn that Lily could not have children. I did not bother to reply."

Stuart knew that this was the kind of thing that his father would do.

Marlon put his hand on Stuart's arm. "It must not have been easy for you," he said. "I know how my brother could be, and I know that he would have wanted you to redeem our family name at any cost."

Stuart was very uncomfortable and he wanted to take his arm away, but he felt it would look too suspicious. He was still having a difficult time trying to keep his thoughts straight.

"I wish that my brother did not go to work for the Duke," said Marlon, making Stuart squirm in his chair. "Men like the Duke imagine that they are God's chosen put here to bring the Kingdom of God to the earth. He obviously never read what our Father said about the Kingdom of God, or he would know that it's already here and always has been here."

Now Stuart was worried. Why would he bring up the Duke? Did he suspect? What did he mean about the Kingdom of God?

"The Duke is the biggest fool of them all," declared Marlon, taking his hand from Stuart's arm. "He wanted me to work for him, and only settled for my brother. He believed that I was the one to finally make his greatest dream come true." Marlon turned and looked Stuart in the eye. "Do you know what his dream is?"

"No, I do not," Stuart answered. He was now almost forgetting about his plan of deception, and wanted only to hear what his uncle would say next.

Marlon began to laugh. "He wants to breed himself a new Christ."

Stuart was shocked by what he had just heard. He had never considered this before.

"He wants to breed a new Christ the same way he breeds himself a good hunting dog," Marlon shook his head. "I was to be one of his breeders. I was to be his pride pedigree dog. Can you imagine that my son? How can any man be so stupid?"

"Well, I suppose we all want Jesus back," said Stuart, feeling conflicted and confused.

"Of course we do," Marlon patted Stuart's arm, "but to be so arrogant as to think that you can breed a new Him. And what does the Duke imagine he would do with a new Christ? The rich and powerful didn't like Him at all. It amazes me that the Duke and others like him could think that they are any different from Herod, or Caiaphas, or Pilate just because they say 'Oh Jesus, blah blah blah' on Sundays. They are the same sort of men.

"And furthermore, what do they know about the soul? Even if they had a scientist, who had figured out how to physically recreate Jesus Christ, what is the body without the soul to power it? Do they decide upon the soul? Do they know how to properly nurture the soul? They know nothing! It is always God's world, my son, and those who are arrogant enough to believe they can control it are pathetic and delusional. Men like the Duke are complete and utter fools!"

Stuart sat in silence. He wanted to say something. He wanted to answer in some way, but he was so stunned by all he had heard that there were no words to help. For the first time, Stuart was feeling real regret that he had agreed to take on this job. What if his uncle was right? What if all he had been raised to believe was wrong? What if the Duke really were just a fool?

# 7

Rose sat in the empty church and waited. Her mother told her to sit there while she went to speak with the Reverend in his office. Reverend Irving was the one who had hired her mother as a cleaner. It was he who had eventually convinced her to join, and it was also he who had helped her to quit drinking.

Rose was not sure how she felt about Reverend Irving. From the outside, he seemed very sincere in his efforts to help her mother. He was always soft-spoken and smiling. She knew her mother thought highly of him. It was always 'Reverend Irving this' and 'Reverend Irving that.' Sometimes Rose wondered if Jeannie wanted to marry him from the way she talked. The Reverend did not have a wife, even though he was not a young man.

Rose straightened the hymn books in front of her and tapped the floor with her running shoes. She was getting very tired of waiting. Finally, she could sit no more and went to see if her mother was almost through. Rose stood outside the open door of the Reverend's office. She could see her mother kneeling on the floor with her eyes closed and her head down. Reverend Irving was standing opposite her with one hand on her head and the other in the air. He was praying loudly, and Rose could hear every word.

"In the name of Jesus Almighty, I pray that this day is a day of healing for this lost sinner! Get out Satan! By the power of Jesus, be gone! No longer torture this poor pathetic woman! Out! Out! I command you! By the power given to me through the Blood of Christ, I demand that you, Satan, be banished back behind the gates of hell!

Rose just stood and watched as Reverend Irving continued to pray over her mother. She had seen this kind of praying many times before, but this time there was something different. Something about it was making her cringe in disgust. Wanting to, but unable to turn away, she suddenly realized what was making her feel the way she did. It was all about Reverend Irving's eyes. His eyes were not closed in prayer like her mother's. Instead, they were wide open. They were wide open and staring at a picture on the wall. In the picture was Jesus with pale white skin and long flowing blond hair. He was wearing a silky blue robe and his bright red lips were unsmiling beneath his neatly trimmed beard. He stood with his back straight and his right hand on the head of a kneeling African woman dressed in rags. The Reverend never once looked away from this picture. It was then that Rose knew, despite Reverend Irving's constant smile and soothing voice, he could never be trusted.

The next three days went well for Stuart. He was spending most of his time helping Marlon in the garden. There were flowers to tend, fledgling vegetables to care for and bushes to keep trimmed. It was not hard work, and Stuart found it surprisingly relaxing. There were times when he had to admit that this was turning into a very enjoyable and peaceful rest.

He was now feeling very confident in his ability to gain his uncle's complete trust. After Marlon's outburst on the first day, he made sure to keep their conversations light and friendly. He avoided any more talk of the Bloodline. Not only did he believe that keeping Marlon calm and happy was for the best, but he was also still feeling a little bothered by everything Marlon had said to him. He did not want to hear anything else that could possibly distract him from his mission.

It was already Thursday, and the two were sitting in the garden when Stuart reminded his uncle that he must leave the next day to attend the party. "I will be leaving tomorrow after tea-time," he said. "I am so looking forward to seeing my lovely lady, again. One day Uncle Marlon, I would very much like you to meet her. She is so very delicate—a truest rose in every sense."

"Stuart," said Marlon.

"Yes Uncle, what is it?" asked Stuart, prepared to come up with a quick answer to any question about this girl. The truth was that he had met her only briefly once before and they had barely exchanged a word.

"Stop it!" Marlon suddenly shouted, making Stuart jump in his chair.

Shocked that his uncle had yelled at him, Stuart did not know what to say. Eventually he stammered, "P-pardon me?"

In a much calmer voice, Marlon said, "Good God Stuart, you don't love that girl. You don't love any girl."

"What are you saying Uncle? Why would you say such a horrible thing?"

"Well, perhaps I say it Stuart because you are a homosexual. That just may have something to do with it."

Stuart was aghast. No one had ever said this to him openly, and certainly not like that. "How can you say such a thing?"

"Because it is true," said Marlon, looking Stuart straight in the eye.

Stuart looked right back at him and said defiantly, "I assure you that I have had sex with a woman before, and she was extremely pleased."

"Oh, I am certain she was," said Marlon, "as I am certain that you put a great deal of effort into the entire affair. However, did it change you Stuart? Did it make you stop needing men?"

At first, Stuart did not know how to reply to this. He still wanted to deny it, but what could he possibly say? Marlon had somehow discovered his secret and there was no point in trying to keep it hidden any longer. He simply gave in and said sadly, "Is it that obvious?"

Marlon smiled, "No Stuart, it's not. You're very practiced at hiding the truth. However, your skills for hiding the truth are no match for my skills of uncovering it. There were a number of clues. The most annoying of which was the way you always talked about Lady Alexa as if you were reading from a Jane Austen novel."

Stuart smiled with embarrassment and looked down at his ring. "Oh Uncle," he said, "I just did not want you to know. It is my sin to bear."

"And is that how you see yourself—as a sinner?"

"According to the Book of Leviticus, I am," he answered.

"Have you read that book through?" asked Marlon. "Why if that book is right and you are damned, then we certainly all are. Have you read all of those insane rules? Not only are we all damned, but it would also mean that God Almighty is as mad as a hatter."

Stuart laughed a little.

"Don't get me wrong," Marlon continued. "The Bible is of great value, but you must read it with a grain of salt. Think about it. It starts off with everything being terribly good and then suddenly everything goes terribly wrong. After that, we have murders, tribal divisions, wars, brutality, and the nightmare of women being reduced to pieces of property. I would have to conclude that everything you read after the point where things go awry is suspect. This would most certainly include the Book of Leviticus."

Stuart was amazed. He had never even considered this, having always been taught that the law was the law.

"To better understand who we are, let's look outside the Bible, and only at what is," said Marlon. "Do you know what happens when a person is completely isolated without any human contact?"

Stuart thought about it for a minute, and then said, "I suppose that person would go mad."

"And why is that?"

"Severe loneliness can drive people insane, as I understand it."

"Yes, but why?" asked Marlon. "Why does this happen? Why can people not live a completely isolated existence?"

Stuart thought about it some more, but this time could not come up with an answer. "I do not know," he said.

"It is because human beings intensely need each other. We long desperately for each other, and when we do not have each other, we can no longer survive. We need each other the same way we need food, or water, or air. It is in our nature to be nourished by one another. When we do not receive this, our minds die, which chokes our very souls."

Stuart had never thought of this before, but he could see that it was true.

"But humans are so very complicated and our relationships are so varied. There are many levels and types of intimacy, but the most important we will ever know is the need to take a mate. This somehow strikes at the very core of who we are. So what does it mean Stuart if your need for a mate is for someone of the same sex?"

"I am not sure, Uncle. Sometimes I think that I might one day wake up and feel differently."

"Oh Stuart," sighed Marlon, "if you were going to change, surely your little carnal adventure with that lady would have done the trick."

Stuart laughed and said, "I suppose it would have."

"I have seen men who, despite what their heart needed, married a woman anyway and it was disastrous. Such men become angry and capable of such cruelty; and the women always suffer a lifetime of broken heartedness. Promise me that you will never do that, Stuart. Never marry a woman when that is not who you are."

Marlon did not wait for a reply, instead he continued talking. "Anyway, as I was saying, you cannot change this, and how or why it happened is irrelevant. It is just something that is in your very foundation. Your deep spiritual need for a mate is within the realm of the masculine, and that is just the way it is.

"Now, I would like to ask you the serious question of whether or not this relationship is capable of true love. Not just an infantile obsession or mindless lust, but real love between equal and mature partners. I know that for me, a man with a need for women, it can be about love—but what about you, Stuart? Is it about real love?"

Stuart thought about it. He thought about Jack. Jack was pudgy, plain and from Liverpool. Stuart began to smile and thought to himself, *it must be love*. "Yes Uncle," he said, "yes, I suppose it is about love."

"Then, how can it possibly be a sin?" said Marlon. "You know that love is always the first commandment of Our Father Jesus. It is the one sure thing that can bring us closer to Him."

Stuart felt a sudden surge of mixed emotions well up within him. His first thought was to try and bring it under control, but he could not stop it. All he could do was to cover his face and try his best not to sob too loudly. The entire thing was just too much. Until that moment, no one outside of Jack had ever made him feel that he was not just some horrible mistake of nature. When he felt his uncle's hand on his shoulder, he was suddenly no longer worried about how he must look and sound. At that point, he moved his hands from his face, and grabbed Marlon's hand. Tears continued to fall as he held on tightly. Stuart could no longer think. All he could do was to continue to purge the hurt and pain he had kept buried for so long.

# 8

Stuart was in his room busily packing when his uncle appeared in the doorway. "I trust that you still intend to return and finish your vacation. I have enjoyed these past few days, and I would like to continue to know you better." said Marlon.

"Oh, you cannot be rid of me now, Uncle. I will be back tomorrow morning," said Stuart, who was sincerely looking forward to returning.

"So, you will still be taking Lady Alexa to the party?" asked Marlon.

Stuart closed the lid of his valise and zipped it shut. "As I have already promised, I cannot now just abandon her. That would not be right."

"I suppose it would not," said Marlon, who sat down in a chair near the door. He looked at Stuart and asked, "One thing that I neglected to ask you yesterday, is whether or not there is someone special in your life. Is there someone?"

Stuart was caught off guard by his uncle's question. By sharing this information with Marlon, he would be opening yet another new door between them. He was already at a point where he did not know what to do next. After all, he was still there on assignment from the Duke. Stuart was deeply confused and unsure if it would be wise to answer the question truthfully.

Marlon gave up waiting and simply said, "Well if there is, tell him that he is welcome here also. I would love to have you both stay for a while."

Stuart did not expect this at all. He had come to terms with the fact that, even though Jack's mother knew about him and they had talked on the phone, there would never be anyone on his side who would accept Jack. "Yes Uncle," he said, without thinking twice about his answer, "his name is Jack, and I am sure that he would love to meet you."

Marlon smiled. "Well, then I will be looking forward to seeing you and Jack tomorrow."

* * *

It was a warm and sunny day, as Rose walked along the wooded path. The trees were full of singing birds, and a song she once heard on the radio kept playing in her head. The entire world was filled with music. Most of that morning had been spent sitting upon her favorite rock by the river, and enjoying the beauty of everything around her. It was now almost noon, and she was headed home for lunch.

As she continued down the path, it seemed as if the day would be full of nothing but good things, then without any warning, she heard the sound of voices from behind her. Rose looked back and saw Glen and two of his friends coming out of the trees.

At first they did not notice her, and seemed to be going in the other direction. Then one of them looked back and shouted, "Hey!" Rose saw Glen turn and look straight at her. He grinned and shouted, "*Injun* on the warpath! Git her!"

Without a second thought, Rose began to run. She had never won any races at school, and knew immediately that it would take all she had to escape the three boys. Not wasting any time by looking back, she ran as fast as she could. Despite how hard she tried, it was not long before she could hear the boys starting to close in. She veered off into the woods to try and lose them. She kept running and darting through the trees and the underbrush. She tried to change direction to catch them off-guard and escape. By the time she realized that she had gone the wrong way, it was too late. She was already backed up against the edge of a cliff with the three boys blocking any exit.

"I know karate," said Glen, kicking in the air. The others followed his lead and eagerly kicked in the air also.

In fear and confusion, Rose took a small step back. Her foot came down on empty space, and she began to fall backwards through the air. As she fell, time slowed to a crawl, revealing every fraction of every second. Then, it was as if the world stopped entirely. As she floated in that timeless space, a peculiar thing happened. She could not be sure whether she grabbed hold of a tree branch, or if the tree branch grabbed hold of her, but she found herself swinging slowly and gently to solid ground. Once her feet hit the earth, time began to move at its regular pace once again. Rose looked down at her body to make sure everything was alright. A small scratch on her hand was all she could see.

She looked up at the cliff edge and saw the three boys looking down at her. They stood silent and confused. Rose did not hesitate to remain there any longer. She turned and took off running home.

* * *

As Stuart put his key in the lock, he could hear the modern music playing on the other side of the door. Jack loved American-style music, and had an extensive record collection. Stuart had tried to get him interested in opera, but Jack said that it just did not have the same magic as rock and roll. Sometimes Stuart wondered if he just may be right.

When Stuart entered the room, Jack reached over and turned down the volume of the stereo.

"Hello Stuart. I missed you," he said smiling.

Stuart set down his valise near the door. "I missed you too." He then added, "But I can't stay long. I have to get ready and attend the Duke's party. He does not like people to arrive after him."

Jack was no longer feeling so happy. "I wish you did not have to go. Isn't Alexa Spence too young for you anyway? She can't be more than sixteen."

"She just turned eighteen." Stuart went over and sat beside Jack on the sofa. "And I already told you that you have nothing to worry about. This date means nothing. It is simply part of the job."

Jack knew that Stuart was not lying, but he still wished that he did not have to go.

"Forget about that party," said Stuart. "I have some good news to tell you. Uncle Marlon knows about you and has invited you to return with me tomorrow."

At first, Jack could not believe his ears. When he finally realized that it was true, he threw his arms around Stuart's neck and exclaimed, "*I have seen a medicine that's able to breathe life into a stone.*"

This was such welcome news for Jack. Lately, there had been an increasing number of days when he worried that Stuart would buckle under the pressure and leave him. From things Stuart had told him, he understood that, although the Bloodline tolerated some degree of homosexuality within their own group, they would still expect Stuart to marry and not associate with an outsider like Jack. Their relationship had always been like living in a sort of limbo, where anything could happen. The fact that now someone related to Stuart was both accepting and welcoming was a milestone.

Jack jumped up from the sofa. "I'm going off to pack now. Of course, I need to return Sunday night as I must be back at work

Monday morning. Oh, I wish I could stay longer, but I know they would not give me time off on such short notice."

Jack had an office manager's job at an insurance company. Stuart had told him to quit and he would take care of the bills, but Jack insisted on working.

"Stuart, I cannot wait to meet your uncle. Perhaps, this summer we could finally make the trip to Liverpool, and you could meet my mother face to face. She so wants to meet you."

Stuart was delighted to see Jack this happy. "Yes, we will definitely go to Liverpool this summer. I promise."

"To that, I can only say, *to liberty, and not to banishment,*" laughed Jack, as he left the room.

Now sitting alone on the sofa, Stuart's smile dissolved into worry.  He began to think about the evening ahead and what he would say to the Duke. Things were not working out the way he had planned. He was supposed to be a disconnected cold-hearted spy. He was supposed to be tricking an old man into divulging secrets. He was not supposed to be feeling like a loving nephew who was looking forward to introducing the most important person in his life to his uncle. Stuart put his hand to forehead. He had no idea what he was going to do.

# 9

The impressive baroque furnishings and masterful artwork filled the grand parlor to excess. It was obvious to Stuart that this family had no qualms about exhibiting their extreme wealth. He shifted a little on the uncomfortable settee as he waited for Lord Spence to speak. The Lord moved his wheelchair a little closer and looked him up and down. "So Stuart, the Duke says that you are a young man with an impressive future ahead of you. Is this so?" he bluntly asked.

"That is very gracious of the Duke," replied Stuart smiling politely, "and I assure you that I am a man of great ambition."

"That is good news indeed," grinned Lord Spence. "You most certainly do not have the appearance of a nonstarter."

Stuart secretly cringed. That is what they called him in the Public School. Without hesitation, they'd tell him to his face that not only was he a nonstarter, but that he was from an entire family of nonstarters. That one word had the power to instantly slice open old wounds, and turn him into a frightened little schoolboy all over again. Hoping that the Lord did not notice his discomfort, he quietly tried to buck up and push those thoughts out of his mind.

Suddenly, the parlor doors flew open and in walked Lady Spence followed by her daughter Alexa. Alexa was dressed in a floor length Egyptian style dress. It was a rich deep green and trimmed with gold. The neckline was modestly high, and it was sleeveless. Her long blonde hair was piled fashionably on top of her head, and golden globes dangled from her ears.

Stuart politely stood up and bowed to the women. Lord Spence, who was quite capable of standing on his own, chose to remain seated in his wheelchair.

"Now, there is a vision, do you not think so Stuart?" asked Lord Spence, grinning at the sight of his two ladies.

"So much more than a vision," replied Stuart, playing his role as prince charming. He stepped forward, took Alexa's hand and kissed it.

"Good evening Stuart," she sang. "I have been looking forward to us meeting once again."

"As have I, My Lady," said Stuart with a dash of smile.

"Shall we go then?" asked Lady Alexa.

Stuart was happy that she seemed eager to leave. He did not want to remain in that house much longer. He turned to Lord Spence in order to get the nod that it was alright to go. Lord Spence waved his hand and said, "Yes, be off to your party young people. I wish that I too could attend, but my doctor advised against it." Lord Spence had been suffering from heart problems for many years.

Stuart offered Alexa his arm and she gracefully linked her own with his. As they walked past a smiling Lady Spence, they politely said their goodbyes, and headed for the door. Once outside, they walked down the grand steps like a prince and princess from a fairytale. Stuart opened the car door and helped his lady inside. Everything, so far, was going very smoothly.

As they drove out of the gates, Alexa suddenly asked, "Does this thing have a radio?" Then without waiting for an answer, she reached over and turned the knob. The sounds of classical music wafted out of the speakers. "Oh hell!" she exclaimed, and changed the station. Rock and roll music now filled the car. "Groovy!" she said, turning up the volume a little and then sitting back in her seat and bopping her head.

Stuart was taken aback by this unexpected behavior. Unsure how he should deal with it, he simply asked, "You enjoy modern music, My Lady?"

Nothing prepared Stuart for what Alexa said next. She looked over at him and said, "They want us to mate you know."

Stuart was shocked. He had no idea what to say.

"That's right, Stu," said Alexa. "They want us to mate, so why don't you just pull over here, and whip it out. Let's get to it!" Alexa began to laugh hysterically.

Stuart kept his hands on the wheel and his eyes locked on the road. He could not believe what she had just said to him.

Alexa was laughing so hard that she could no longer speak. Finally, she managed to say, "Oh Stu, you should have seen your face. That is the funniest thing I have ever seen. What an old geezer you are. How old are you anyway?"

"Uh…twenty-seven," he said blankly. He was now wondering what he had gotten himself into. This was not the evening he had been expecting.

"Well, that's far too old for me," said Alexa. "My Amando is only eighteen, and he is much more handsome than you. He has hair as black as the night sky, eyes the color of chocolate and skin like sweet brown sugar."

"Who is Amando?" Stuart asked, still unsure how best to deal with this strange situation.

"Oh, he's one of our gardeners," answered Alexa, "and my lover." She began to laugh again. "Surprise! I am not Lady Alexa. I am Lady Chatterley."

Stuart now found himself smiling at her laughter. He had to admit that she was funny. "And why would you tell me this?" he asked.

Alexa leaned over and put her head on his shoulder. "Because you and I, Stu, are two peas in a pod."

Stuart was surprised that she had put her head on his arm, but did not find it uncomfortable at all. "And how is that?" he asked in amusement.

"Because," she continued, "we both have our secret loves. For me, it is my beautiful Spanish gardener, and for you it is…I don't know…some bloke."

Stuart was horrified. How did this girl know about him? He did not know what to say.

Alexa put her hand on his arm, "Don't be upset, Stu," she said gently. "Everyone knows."

Stuart was shocked. "What do you mean everyone knows?"

"Come now, you know how people gossip. Especially those Bloodline people. It's well known that you are…well…you know…you fancy blokes." For a few minutes, there was only quiet except for the pounding beat of the music that continued to pour out of the radio.

"And everyone knows this?" asked Stuart, finally breaking the silence.

"Most everyone," said Alexa.

Stuart was confused. How could his secret be general knowledge? Suddenly, it was as if the world he thought he knew had never been real at all. Trying to make sense of it, he asked, "If so many believe this, why then would your parents have me escort you to this party?"

Alexa took her head from his shoulder and patted his arm. "Well Stu, it's like I said before. They want us to mate. Along with the Duke, they've decided that we have compatible gene pools, and regardless of how either one of us feels they intend that we should marry. They are fully confident that somehow we will manage to breed more of those Bloodline babies."

Stuart looked for a second over at Alexa who was looking back and smiling. He could see from her face that she was dead serious. She leaned over and once again rested her head on his arm. "I like you, Stu," she said. "You're alright."

Stuart was speechless. He just continued to look straight ahead and drive.

* * *

The orchestra played and the beautifully dressed couples whirled around on the ballroom floor. Stuart stood off to the side watching and waiting. Alexa had temporarily run off with some of her girlfriends, but did promise him that she would soon return. He hoped that she would not be too long.

As he admired some of the more skilled dancers, he had to confess to himself that he was having a wonderful time. Normally, by this point in the evening, he would have tired of role playing and would be trying to decide how to cut the evening short. But Alexa knew who he was and didn't care. She had him dancing and laughing all evening long. He was no longer upset about learning the gossip that had been spread about him. None of that seemed to matter tonight.

As Stuart happily stood watching the couples waltz in time to the music, he felt a hand move slowly and firmly over his shoulder. He turned to see the Duke standing beside him. "Good evening Stuart. It looks as though you are having a very good time with our lovely little virgin. The extent of your talent for charm does surprise me sometimes. You almost have me believing that you are enjoying her company."

Stuart tried not to physically cringe at the Duke's touch. "Good evening, Your Grace. It is an excellent party."

"And how are things going with Marlon?" the Duke asked, without removing his hand.

"Very well, Your Grace. I will be returning to his home tomorrow, and he has invited me to stay for the rest of the week," replied Stuart, hoping that he would not ask any more questions about his uncle.

"Wonderful!" said the Duke. "And by the way, you do look very handsome in your tuxedo." He then dragged his hand down Stuart's arm. "I would like for you to accompany me to my rooms. It will not take long. You will soon return to the party."

Stuart felt sick to his stomach, but knew that he had no choice. The Duke would accept no excuses. He turned and began to follow the Duke towards the door. They had almost reached the threshold, when he heard someone call his name.

"Stuart! Oh Stuart, there you are! I have been looking everywhere for you."

Alexa was suddenly right in front of him. She grabbed a hold of his hand and was pulling him back towards the dance floor. As she did this, she maneuvered it so that she stood between him and the Duke. The Duke remained silent in the doorway, and looked annoyed. He was obviously taken off guard, and for a moment did not know what to say.

"Good evening, Your Grace," Alexa sweetly sang, making a small flirtatious curtsy. "I have been looking everywhere for my young man and was almost afraid that I had lost him. Stuart has promised to dance the next waltz with me, and it is just about to begin. Would you be so kind as to excuse him?"

The Duke looked at Stuart and then back at Alexa. He took in a deep breath, sighed and said, "I suppose this can wait. Go on then Stuart, and we will have our discussion some other time."

Alexa grabbed Stuart's hand and pulled him off towards the dance floor. He was still a little disoriented and confused by what had just happened. As they stood in the middle of the ballroom, the band began to play The Blue Danube. Stuart took Alexa in his arms, and she whispered into his ear, "What a filthy, beastly old swine he is! You know, he tried it with me only months ago. Luckily I'm a quick thinker, and was able to feign my woman's time. You know Stu, there are some advantages to being a girl."

Stuart looked into her eyes and suddenly realized that she had not merely appeared by co-incidence. "You…you rescued me," he said, just as the tempo picked up.

"Well someone had to," said Alexa, smiling at him as they whirled around. "Just call me your super girl."

Stuart held her closer. "Maybe I should marry you after all," he joked.

Alexa laughed, "Oh that would be groovy—just you, me and all of our Spanish looking babies."

Stuart quickly twirled her around and then expertly dipped her, which made them both laugh out loud.

# 10

The English drizzle from the early morning had stopped, and the sun now shone over the countryside as the car pulled up in front of Marlon's cottage. Before Jack and Stuart had a chance to remove their luggage from the trunk, Marlon appeared at the open door. "Good morrow gentlemen."

"Good morning uncle," said Stuart cheerfully. "I would like you to meet Jack."

"Jack, it is a pleasure to meet you." Stuart was surprised when, instead of merely shaking his hand, Marlon hugged him.

"And it is very nice to meet you too," replied Jack happily.

Stuart removed their luggage from the car and handed one of the bags to Jack.

"Well, come in—come in," said Marlon, stepping inside the cottage and beckoning for them to enter. Once they were all inside, he closed the door and said to Stuart, "Would you please show Jack the room, and both of you may unpack whilst I fix us some tea."

Stuart did not want to make any assumptions and asked, "Which room will Jack stay in?"

"Oh, did you have a falling out on the way here?"

"No…uh…I just..."

Marlon laughed, "Of course he will stay in your room."

Stuart smiled. He could not remember a time when he felt more welcome.

Jack and Stuart went up the small narrow stairs and entered the flowery room. "So, what do you think?" Stuart asked as he placed his suitcase on the bed.

"Your uncle is a very nice man," said Jack. "And you were right, I love the cottage and this room is charming."

Stuart looked around. "So, you don't mind the flowers…or the women."

"Oh no, not at all. It's a beautiful room. Aren't all of those paintings by Leonardo Da Vinci?"

"Yes they are," replied Stuart. "And you do not mind being surrounded by all of these women."

Jack looked at Stuart and said, "Of course not. *For where is any author in the world, Teaches such beauty as a woman's eye!* They are magnificent!"

"Even Leda?" asked Stuart teasingly.

"Oh yes Stuart! Just look at her. She is stunning in every way."

Stuart began to laugh. "Why Jack," he exclaimed, "this is a side of you that I have never seen before."

"Don't you see," said Jack seriously, "women are so important to men—all men—even men like us. They balance us Stuart. They tell us who we are. Without them, we are just creatures with little dangly bits."

"Little? Speak for yourself," joked Stuart.

Jack laughed. "I am being serious. Women are important to every man's health. Men who are full of anger and fear towards them are sick men. They put themselves in danger of becoming something less than a man. Women protect us from ourselves and make us who we are. It is important to be able to love and respect them openly and honestly."

Stuart was silent as he thought about what Jack had just said. He unzipped his suitcase and removed some clothing, which he set down on the bed. Turning his head, he saw that Jack had not yet opened his valise, but continued to gaze quietly at the print. Stuart set down the white shirt he was holding and moved over to stand beside Jack. The two men stood side by side facing Leda. Stuart had to admit that, after what Jack said, she now seemed different. "You are right," he said, putting his arm around Jack. "She is beautiful—she truly is."

* * *

The three men sat around the kitchen table enjoying the tea and home baked cookies. Marlon and Jack chatted continuously, mostly about country living. Stuart was unusually quiet. All the time he sat there, he could only think about how he was going to tell them about his assignment from the Duke. He knew that it was impossible to go on with the charade, and had actually planned to tell Jack before arriving at the cottage. Somehow, he just never mustered up the courage. In his shame, he could not imagine how they would ever forgive him. Still, the longer he let this go on, the worse it would be.

Finally prepared to confess, Stuart opened his mouth to speak. But before he had a chance to utter a sound, Marlon turned to him and said, "I have a chore for you, my son. I hope you do not mind, but I need you to deliver a basket of vegetables to the widow down the road. I promised them to her today. No need to take the car, as it's only a short distance down. She'll likely also ask you in for a cuppa. Don't be rude and refuse. She is a lonely old soul."

Stuart was extremely relieved that he now had a perfectly good excuse to put off his confession. "Of course I will help," he said eagerly. "How wicked would I be not to assist an elderly woman. Is she your pajama-lady, Uncle?"

"Oh no, she is not my admirer—not at all. The pajama-lady, as you put it, lives in the other direction. Daisy lives just west of here, and without me even suggesting that I was interested, she has already told me that I am far too old for her. She says this despite being six years my senior," laughed Marlon.

Stuart pointed to the basket on the kitchen counter. "Is that it?" he asked, desiring to escape the cottage as soon as possible.

"Yes," replied Marlon, "That's it. Just walk west to the second lane. I'll phone ahead to let her know that you are

63

coming. Jack, you may stay here with me so that we may get to know each other better. Stuart should be able to handle this undertaking on his own.”

Stuart picked up the basket. A walk alone sounded like a very good idea right now. Perhaps it would give him time to think of the best way to tell Jack and Marlon the truth. As he headed out through the back door, Marlon exclaimed after him, “And be careful, Stuart. Daisy is seventy-five, but she still thinks that she is twenty-five. Don’t let her sneak up behind you.”

Stuart just laughed at his uncle’s strange humor and went out the door.

Rose and Jeannie sat in the pew waiting for the service to begin. Reverend Irving had been away for two weeks now, and Rose could tell that her mother was looking forward to seeing him in the pulpit again. That morning, Jeannie was singing as they prepared for church. This was a sure sign that she was feeling exceptionally happy.

Reverend Irving suddenly appeared from the side door, and Rose noticed her mother smiling from ear to ear. He walked over and stood in front of the plain wooden podium.

Triumphantly raising his hands, he declared, “This is a glorious morning, good sheep of Jesus!”

“Praise the Lord!” shouted someone from the back.

“Hallelujah!” shouted another.

Reverend Irving lowered his arms and smiled at his congregation. “Before we begin today, I have a very important announcement to make.”

The room was silent as they all waited in anticipation to hear what he had to say.

“As y’all know, I have been away. I have been away visiting old friends and family back home. It was a glorious thing to see faces I have not seen in a very long time, and I must confess, I enjoyed a lot of fine Southern food.” He patted his round stomach and the congregation laughed.

"Well, praise Jesus!" he happily exclaimed. "I have brought back a surprise for y'all." The Reverend paused and the congregation wondered. Suddenly, he waved his hand in the air and shouted, "Come on out, surprise!"

From the side door, appeared a smiling woman dressed in a sky-blue skirt suit. She wore a matching pill box hat, white blouse and white high heels. Her mid-length blond hair was professionally curled and her lips shimmered with red lipstick. The color on her eyelids matched her suit perfectly. She walked towards the Altar, giving a friendly wave of her white gloved hand to the congregation.

Reverend Irving took her hand and had her stand beside him at the podium. He then turned to his flock said, "It is now my pleasure to present to you, Mrs. Irving!" At first, there was only silence as the surprised group tried to grasp this unexpected news.

Suddenly, the room burst into applause. "Praise Jesus!" they shouted with delight. Some of them began to pray out loud.

Rose was afraid to even look over at her mother. She knew that this had sliced her heart wide open, and could now feel Jeannie's intense pain. All around her, people were still happily celebrating, but she could only see her mother's hands firmly clenched in raw anguish. Rose wanted to grab hold of one of those hands and take her mother out of there, but she knew it was not possible. They would both have to sit through the entire sermon.

For the ending hymn that morning, they sang *Take My Hand Precious Lord*. Rose glanced over at her mother who sang with tears rolling down her face. The people who noticed were pleased to see Jeannie so full of the spirit of God. Rose had to look away. She knew that those tears were as far from tears of joy as you could ever get.

* * *

Stuart walked through the back door and into the kitchen. He had a look of shock on his face. "Uncle!" he exclaimed, "I thought that you were only joking when you warned me about Daisy."

Marlon and Jack both burst out laughing.

"You were gone for almost two hours," said Marlon. "We thought about sending in a rescue party after the first hour, but then thought it better to let you fight your way out like a man." The two burst out laughing again.

Stuart was at first a little indignant as he realized that he had been made the fool, but he soon found the laughter too contagious. He tried to hold back a smile and said, "It is not at all amusing. When I arrived there, do you realize that she was wearing a very tight mini-dress?"

"Yes, Daisy does take pride in dressing at the height of fashion," said Marlon.

"Well you certainly have to admire a woman who takes pride in her appearance," Jack added.

"Yes, indeed," said Marlon, with a conspiratorial wink at Jack.

"Well that is certainly not the worst of it," said Stuart. "Do you know that she had me trapped in her pantry for about twenty minutes?"

Marlon and Jack just laughed louder.

"Stop your laughing!" said Stuart, barely able to hold back the laughter himself. "She was blocking the door, and I only finally managed to get out by squeezing through, but not without having to rub up against her."

Jack was now buckled over and clutching his stomach.

"This is not the least bit amusing!" shouted Stuart playfully. "She touched my bum—and more than once!" he added.

The three men were laughing so hard, they could hardly catch their breath. Stuart had to grab a chair and sit down. As their laughter began to subside, something unexpected happened. Stuart suddenly slammed his fist on the table and shouted, "I do not deserve to be so happy!"

Marlon and Jack immediately stopped laughing and looked at him.

Stuart had his head down. "I have done a terrible thing," he said. "I have lied to both of you, and now I will not blame you if you want me to be out of your lives completely."

There was a moment of silence as Stuart tried to think about where to begin. Realizing that there was no good way to deliver the truth, he said, "Uncle Marlon, I did not find you in order to fulfill my father's dying wish of reconciliation. I…I came to deceive you. I do not work for an advertising agency. I work for the Duke, as my father did. He required valuable information that he believes you possess. It was my job to gain your trust and obtain it from you."

"And you Jack,' he said, "I kept this from you, and led you to believe that I was just innocently reconnecting with my long lost uncle. I am so sorry to both of you, and if you hate me, then I fully understand."

Marlon stood up. The expression on his face was now stern and angry. "Well, if you have spoken to the Duke, then you must know that I am part of the Underground. And you should also know, Stuart, that the Underground does not take these sorts of things lightly."

Marlon moved over to a sideboard and slowly opened the drawer. "There is only one way we deal with this sort of deception." He reached his hand inside and then in one sudden movement he flung something white across the table. It hit Stuart right in the face. Jack burst out laughing.

"Your freshly washed underpants Mr. MI6," said Marlon, making Jack laugh even louder. "Did you think that just because I am an old man living on my own, I would never clean under my furniture?"

Stuart was in shock. For a few moments, he didn't know what to think. He just sat looking blankly at the underwear in his hand. Finally, he began to realize what was happening. "You…you knew?" he asked of his uncle.

"Of course I knew," smiled Marlon. "You are a terrible spy, and your story about your father wanting to reconcile with me was an obvious fabrication. He may have had something to say about me on his death bed, but it certainly would not be words of reconciliation."

Jack put his hand on Stuart's back and said, "While you were busy with your new girlfriend, Uncle Marlon filled me in on a few things. I knew that something was afoot, but I had faith that you would eventually tell me."

Stuart was still shocked by it all. "And neither one of you is angry with me?" he asked in amazement.

Marlon looked him in the eye and said, "We have all done things that we now regret, Stuart. Jack and I understand that you are a man who has wrestled hard with the demons life has handed you. We both have faith that you are a good and decent human being. Jack here loves you deeply, and in the short time that we have known each other, I must say that I have become very fond of you. While you were out, we discussed many things, including how we both understand and forgive you."

Stuart could not believe what he had just heard. Tears came to his eyes as he decided that from then on everything had to change. "No matter what happens," he said, "I promise that I will never deceive either of you again. You have my word, and it will never be broken."

# 11

Rose had changed from her Sunday dress to her shorts and t-shirt. She stood on the large boulder in her backyard, and looked at the sky. Birds of many kinds were soaring overhead. Some of them were so high that they became just tiny specks, and she could not tell whether they might be crows or robins. She watched as a sparrow flew low, dipped and turned on the wind. Birds were lucky. They could go wherever they wanted unhindered by the earth.

Rose closed her eyes and thought that maybe if she tried really hard, she too could fly like a bird. She put her arms straight out and felt the wind blowing against them. Taking in a deep breath, she began to move her arms up and down, up and down, as fast as she could. Then she bent her legs and pushed off from the rock. Instead of flying gracefully upward, she came down hard on the ground below. Sitting in the grass, she looked up with longing at the birds that flew effortlessly over her head.

As she rested there a moment, a big black crow suddenly came swooping down and then back up again, landing on the roof of the house. He remained perched there in silent stillness. Something was wrong! Rose looked at the backdoor and knew that something was terribly wrong! She got up and ran as fast as she could. Throwing open the old wooden screen door, she then stopped just inside of the kitchen.

Jeannie, who was sitting at the table, quickly hid something behind her back. Rose did not see the thing clearly, but she did not have to see it. She knew exactly what her mother was hiding.

Rose looked straight into her mother's eyes which she could see were red and swollen from crying. Without thinking twice about it, she loudly exclaimed, "Mama, I don't want to go to that church no more!"

Jeannie was so worried that Rose may have seen the bottle that she did not really hear what her daughter had said. Instead of responding, she only stared in silent confusion.

Rose slowly moved a little closer to her mother. "I don't like that church! I don't like Reverend Irving! And I'm not going ever again!"

Jeannie looked down at the table in front of her. Her heart was full of shame—shame for her thoughts about Reverend Irving—shame that she did not look and dress like Mrs. Irving—shame that no man would love and want to marry a poor colored woman. She looked up at Rose and sadly said, "But then we will go to hell. Do you want to go to hell?"

Rose stood at her mother's side. "They lied Mama! They said our hearts would turn black. They said that it is a good thing for Lot to offer his daughters to evil men. They lied!"

Jeannie looked into her daughter's eyes and found that she could not look away.

Rose reached over and gently touched her mother's hand. "But they didn't lie when they said that Jesus and God loves us Mama. That's something they didn't lie about. But God and Jesus won't send us to hell just 'cause we don't go to that church. That's a big lie! Reverend Irving is a liar! Mama, God loves you, and isn't a big stupid meanie like they say."

As Jeannie looked into Rose's eyes, it was impossible not to see the scar on her daughter's forehead. What had she been thinking? That could not happen again. She knew she could not let that happen again. Jeannie felt her heart begin to beat louder and stronger. "You know what?" she said, with a slight smile. "I was looking for the dustpan in the cellar and I found this." Jeannie took the bottle from behind her back and showed it to Rose.

"We missed one—didn't we Mama?" Rose said.

"Yes we did," replied Jeannie. The dark feelings that had consumed her since the church service that morning quickly dissolved away, and she was suddenly aware of how bright the sun was shining through the windows.

"Can I go pour it out?" Rose held out her hand for the bottle.

Jeannie smiled. "Go and pour it where you poured the others."

Rose took the bottle in hand and headed for the door. As she opened it, she turned back to Jeannie and asked, "We don't have to go to that church no more, right?"

"No Sugar," answered her mother, "we're not going there no more."

"Good," said Rose. She paused for a second and then added, "Jesus loves us Mama. I know it's the truth." She then turned and went out to empty the last bottle.

✳ ✳ ✳

It was Sunday morning, and the three men sat together relaxing in the garden. The sun was shining warm, and they were silently enjoying nature's melodic sounds of summer. Marlon did not want to break their peaceful meditation, but he knew that the subject had to be addressed. Nothing more had been said about the Duke since Stuart's confession, and there was no point in putting it off any longer.

"You are aware that you will not be able to simply pack it in," he said to Stuart.

Stuart did not have to ask Marlon what he was talking about. He understood exactly what he meant. "I realize that, Uncle, and I have been thinking a great deal about it."

"You are likely in it, as some would say, for the long haul," said Marlon.

"I understand completely, and I am prepared to do whatever you feel is best. I need both your advice and your guidance." Stuart turned to Jack and said, "Perhaps you should go for a walk, Jack. I do not want to drag you into this."

Jack recognized that Stuart was only concerned about his safety. "I'm sorry," he said, "but I am not going anywhere. Whatever is going to happen will affect me no matter what, and I, at the very least, want the chance to help as much as I can. I am not afraid Stuart, and I will not turn my back on you."

Stuart was about to argue with Jack, but Marlon spoke up first, "He is correct, my son. If it involves you, then it involves Jack also. It is neither fair nor right that you should keep him at a distance. You must share your burdens together."

Stuart looked at Jack who knowingly looked back at him. "Yes, of course" said Stuart, "I suppose that I am just accustomed to always keeping things neatly partitioned in my life. I am sorry Jack. I would be grateful for any help you can provide."

"Thank you, Stuart," said Jack, reaching over and touching his hand. "I just want to help you."

Marlon leaned forward in his chair a little and asked Stuart, "What exactly does the Duke want from me? What does he believe I have?"

"He says that you may have secret information," replied Stuart. "He wanted me to befriend you, and somehow learn the secrets you were possibly hiding."

"And what is the nature of these secrets?" asked Marlon.

"It has something to do with locating a golden child from the Bloodline—a child that would one day change the world. He said that it is prophesied within the Fatima visions."

Marlon's eyes opened wider. "The Fatima visions!" he exclaimed.

"Yes, he has documents sent to him from a newly formed Catholic agency. These documents have to do with the third prophecy of Fatima. The prophecy included information about a child who would bring about great change in the world."

Marlon sat back in his chair and closed his eyes. For the longest time, he did not say a thing, and then a single tear ran down his cheek.

Stuart waited in silence for his uncle to explain. Finally, he could no longer hold back and asked, "Do you know about the Fatima prophecy regarding such a child?"

Marlon opened his eyes and smiled. "No, I did not know. Although there have been many other signs that a special child would not only come, but that she has already arrived. To hear you say what you did assures me that it is truly happening. I am feeling such hope and joy right now, that I cannot think straight. Give me a moment to gather my thoughts."

Stuart looked at his uncle's face and suddenly felt like maybe there was a reality to it all. Although he had spent a great deal of time looking for this child, it had always been just another work assignment. He didn't truly believe in what he was searching for. It was simply another meaningless task in a meaningless world. Marlon's reaction made him begin to wonder if this was something important. What if this was the most important thing to ever happen in his life?

Marlon looked over at Stuart and asked, "Have you seen the papers on the prophecy?"

"No," he replied, "The Duke did not allow me to see them."

"We must find out what is written there," said Marlon. "Those papers will hold vital clues that are necessary to find her."

It was at this point that Stuart realized that he was now working for his uncle. Without hesitation he said, "I think I know where he would keep them."

Marlon looked at Stuart. "You know that this is very serious business. If you work against the Duke, it will be dangerous. If he finds out, he will likely not hesitate to have you killed, Stuart. I want you to fully understand what it could mean to you and to Jack."

Stuart worriedly looked over at Jack. "I'm not afraid of that miserable old goat," said Jack, defiantly. "I think we should do what we have to."

Stuart smiled at Jack's confidence. "Well, if Jack is not afraid, then neither am I."

Marlon looked at them both. "As long as you both understand what we will be facing…"

Jack spoke up before Stuart could respond, "We are not cowards, Marlon. If this is important to the greater good, then we are prepared to make whatever sacrifices are necessary. We shall *fight to the last gasp*."

Stuart looked at Jack and felt proud. This was why he could not help but love him.

Marlon turned to Stuart and asked, "Could you get hold of those Fatima papers? I realize that the Duke is very careful about security, and it may not be easy."

"I…," Stuart hesitated for a second, "As his personal assistant, my office is in his home. I have special access to the house and…and I have knowledge of his private rooms."

Marlon sensed tension in the air between Stuart and Jack. He did not have to guess why. There was little he did not know about his old enemy the Duke.

"I am quite certain that he would keep these papers in the cabinet where he keeps everything of great personal importance to him," continued Stuart. "It should be no problem to get hold of these documents, as long as he is out of the house."

Marlon looked intensely at his nephew and said, "I wish that I did not have to ask you to do this, but I don't believe we have a choice. The stakes are greater than either one of us could ever imagine. The Duke will go to any lengths to find that child. We must find her first."

Stuart could see that this would be a difficult task and began to feel a little self-doubt. "Uncle, I will promise to try as best I can to help. However, as you yourself said, I am no spy. I just hope that I do not make everything worse."

Marlon reached over and touched Stuart's arm. "You may not be much of a secret agent," he said, "but maybe Robin Hood is more your style."

Jack smiled, "I think Robin Hood is exactly who you are, Stuart."

Stuart raised his eyebrows and replied, "If either one of you thinks that I will be putting on a pair of tights, then you had best think again."

As Jack and Marlon laughed, Stuart leaned back in his chair and closed his eyes. Except for the sounds of the birds, everything was now silent. He could feel the warm reassuring sun on his face as he drank in the soothing country breeze. *Robin Hood*, he laughed in his mind, *if I am to get through this, then perhaps Sir Robin Hood is who I will have to be.*

# 12

Rose quickly ate up the last few peas left on her plate. Today was her birthday, and all she could think about was the cake and the present that would come next. She turned to her mother and waited impatiently for her to finish. It seemed to take forever, but Jeannie eventually took the final bite of her supper.

"Are you done?" asked Rose eagerly.

Jeannie smiled at Rose's excitement. "Are you sure you have room for cake?" she asked teasingly.

"I always have room for cake," answered Rose, quickly picking up the two empty plates and setting them on the kitchen counter.

Without another word, Jeannie went to the fridge and took out the small white frosted homemade cake. *Happy Birthday Rose* was written in green and red icing on the top. She set it down on the table and put in eight brand new birthday candles of various colors. Jeannie then lit each one with a wooden match.

Rose gazed at the beautiful fiery cake, while her mother sang *Happy Birthday*. She knew it would soon be time to make a wish. This was a very important part of a birthday. This was the one time in the whole year where you got to have a wish of your very own. She began to think hard about what it was that she really wanted. There were many things that she could ask for, but Rose could only think of one thing she wanted the most.

More than anything else, she just wanted to sit in the middle of a big field of flowers.

"Okay," said Jeannie, "time to blow 'em out."

Rose closed her eyes. She saw the field—she saw the big, tall, beautiful flowers—and then in the middle of it all she saw herself. Taking in a deep breath, she blew as hard and as long as she could. The candles all went out on the first try. Rose was thrilled! If they all go out on the first blow, it means that your wish will definitely come true.

Jeannie then stepped over to the cupboard and removed a box wrapped in colorful paper. She felt some hesitation about giving it to Rose. With her no longer working at the church, she did not have as much money as before. She had found this in the bargain bin. It was one of the many toys that did not sell well the Christmas before and had been marked down to cost or below.

Rose looked eagerly at the present. She took it in her hands and said, "Thank you Mama." Slowly and carefully, she unwrapped the gift. It was a brightly colored box with a cellophane front. Through the clear plastic she could see a little doll that was different from any she had seen before. She already had two dolls that were similar to this. Jeannie had purchased them second hand from the Salvation Army Store, but this doll was definitely different.

Rose read the name on the box. It said *Julia* with a small heart dotting the 'i'. Julia was not dressed in fancy clothes like the other dolls. Instead she wore a plain white nurse's uniform with a cap and white shoes. Her skin was brown, and her dark hair was short. Rose looked at her face in amazement. This was the most beautiful face she had ever seen!

"Do you like it," asked Jeannie anxiously.

Rose looked at her mother. "It's the best doll ever!' she exclaimed, throwing her arms around her mother's neck. "Thank you Mama," she added, kissing her mother's cheek.

Jeannie was very relieved.

"Can I take her out of the box?" Rose asked.

"Well, it's no good keeping her in there," said Jeannie. "Go ahead."

Rose opened the top of the box and took out her new doll. She touched the thick crisp uniform with its tiny white buttons. She took off the little white shoes and then put them back on. She stroked the soft hair under the cap. Julia was brand new and perfect in every way.

There was one peculiar thing Rose noticed about Julia. On her uniform, above the left breast was a small shiny gold button or pin. At first, Rose wondered what it could be, when suddenly she knew exactly what it was. *That*, she thought to herself, *is the mark of the golden heart. It must mean that Julia has a heart of gold.* Rose had heard of people having hearts of gold and understood that it meant that they were very special people. Julia was certainly very special.

After they enjoyed the cake, Rose looked out of the window and could see that there was still plenty of sunlight. She just loved the magic of long summer evenings. The soft sounds and fresh smells were so comforting. Also, all of the colors changed with the sinking sun, making it look like a wonderful new dream world. Today was her birthday, so it was even more important than ever to go outside. She turned to her mother and asked, "Can I go out and play? It's still light."

Jeannie looked at the clock and saw that it was fourteen minutes after seven. "Just for a little while," she said. "But if it starts getting dark, you come home."

Rose was thrilled. "I'm taking Julia with me," she said, grabbing her doll and letting the screen door slam behind her.

Once outside, Rose began to run. She did not know where she was going, but there was something in the air that made her feel like she was free to go anywhere. Her hair was flying in the wind, and her feet seemed to be floating on air. She clutched tightly onto Julia, as she felt the drumming rhythm of her own heart.

Turning down the old gravel road, she ran up the hill and past her favorite tree. Still running, she then veered off towards a small open area near where the corn grew. As soon as she was within view of the clearing, she stopped in her tracks. For a moment, Rose could not believe what she was seeing. It was not what she expected. There in front of her were thousands of beautiful wildflowers! They were of all different kinds and colors. She had just been to that very spot only a week ago, and at that time there was nothing but grass and weeds. This was magic!

Excitedly, she ran into the middle and sat down. She turned her head this way and that to see in every direction. Everywhere she looked, she saw nothing but flowers. They were not exactly the perfect flowers with giant petals from her dream. These flowers were crooked and wild, and the petals were much smaller. But, to Rose, it was the most wonderful place she had ever been in her life.

She bent Julia's legs and placed her on the ground within the flower fortress. "Look Julia," Rose said. "This is the birthday gift that God and Jesus sent me. They sent it in my birthday wish. Isn't it beautiful?"

Julia did not reply. She just remained perfectly poised and silent, but her tiny pink lips held the faintest of smiles.

It was Sunday night, and Stuart and Jack were just returning home from their weekend at Marlon's cottage. As they entered the hallway to the flat, they suddenly stopped at the odd sight before them. "There's a Druid on our doorstep," whispered Jack.

Sitting on the carpet in front of their door was a small, hooded figure dressed all in black. The head was bowed, and it looked as though it may be sleeping. Stuart and Jack moved slowly closer, and the figure turned to look at them. Suddenly, it jumped up and rushed towards them. Stuart backed up a little, but just then the creature's hand flew up and pushed back the hood, revealing the girl hiding beneath it. "There you are my beloved betrothed!" exclaimed Alexa, lunging forward and throwing her arms around him.

"Alexa! What a surprise," said Stuart. He nervously looked over at Jack, afraid that he might get the wrong idea. He could see that Jack was not upset at all, but instead look rather amused.

Alexa let go of Stuart and turned to Jack. "I'm Alexa, and who are you short, dark and handsome?"

Before Stuart could introduce them, Jack simply answered, "I'm Jack."

Alexa threw her arms around him and gave him a big hug. "Groovy name! I am so happy to meet you, Jack."

Stuart was already putting his key in the lock. He opened the door and all three went inside.

"Forgive me for showing up on your doorstep unannounced, but I have a favor to ask of you," Alexa said to Stuart. "You see, they are getting suspicious, and I didn't dare phone."

Stuart looked at her, confused by what she was trying to tell him.

Alexa could see that he did not understand. "My parents," she explained, "the Lord and Lady of the manor are becoming suspicious that I may be secretly seeing someone—that I may not be their little Snow White any longer." She then turned to Jack and said, "You see Jack, I am in love with Amando. He is one of our gardeners, so as you can imagine, my parents would not be very happy about it."

Alexa turned back to Stuart. "I need your help. Could you please write me a love letter that I may accidentally leave on my desk? If my parents believe that 'the special someone' I am involved with is you, then they will back off and not have me followed. Since the party, they appear to be even more eager for a match between us."

Alexa looked back at Jack and said, "Again, I apologize for surprising you this evening, but of course I could not phone you on a bugged line."

Stuart was taken aback by what she had just said. "Bugged?" he asked.

"Of course," said Alexa, surprised at Stuart's naivety. "Anyone who works for the Duke would certainly have their phone bugged. Did you never think of that?"

Stuart looked over at Jack, and knew from the expression on his face what he was thinking. Every private phone call they had ever made to each other or to someone else would not have been private at all. It was a terrible violation, and Stuart could feel himself getting angry. Now more than ever, he was determined to undermine the Duke in any way he could.

Stuart looked at Alexa and suddenly had an idea. "It is possible," he said, "that we would be able to help each other. You need me as an excuse to be able to see Amando, and I just realized that I am going to need you to explain some unusual behavior of my own."

Alexa was pleased that Stuart would ask for her help. "Of course I will do anything you need. You are my friend, Stu. Just ask and your wish is my command," she said with a bow.

Stuart smiled at her. "Tomorrow I must go to my office, but the Duke will wonder why I am even in London, as I am supposed to be somewhere else. If I have returned in part to court you, then he should not be suspicious. Could you meet me at my office? You will provide me with the perfect excuse. Also, I will need your help to convince the Duke to leave his home. I have a good idea on how to accomplish this. You see, there are some important papers in his house and I must find them."

"Oh, I dig it!" exclaimed Alexa, who found this proposal very exciting. The thought of deceiving the Duke was extremely appealing. "This could be an awful lot of fun." She slipped her arm through Stuart's and said to Jack. "Do you mind Jack, if Stu and I do a little courting tomorrow?"

Jack laughed, "I'm sure that he could not be in safer hands."

"Alright then," said Stuart, feeling confident that the plan he had in mind would work. "First off, let me get a pen and paper and I shall write you a love letter. How would you like me to begin?"

Alexa smiled mischievously, "Well, it certainly should not be lame. You need to put your whole heart into it, Stu. Why not begin: *My dearest most beautiful and virtuous Alexa, How do I love thee? Let me count the ways you turn me on baby!*" The three of them burst out laughing as Stuart began to write.

* * *

Stuart had been sitting in his office and nervously waiting for what seemed like a very long fourteen minutes. Alexa was to arrive at any moment now, and he sincerely hoped that she would not be late. He needed her help if his idea was going to work. Just as he expected, it did not take long for the Duke to show up at the door. He glared at Stuart in annoyance and with suspicion.

"Why are you here?" he abruptly asked, as he marched into the room. "You should be with the old man, and not wasting valuable time sitting around and doing nothing."

Before Stuart could answer, the front gate buzzed his office. "Lady Alexa Spence is here to see you, Sir" said the voice through the intercom.

Stuart pushed down the speak button and said, "Yes, allow her entry." He then looked at the Duke and began to apologize, "I am so sorry, Your Grace. It is just that Alexa urgently requested to see me today, and so I returned temporarily. If I let her down now, then I may lose her interest. I understand that young women can easily become capricious if they do not receive proper attention."

The Duke smiled. He was feeling a little proud of Stuart's ambition, and after all, this was a match he had recently sanctioned. "Of course I understand. This is a good choice for you. Her family has the status and fortune that a clever young man should aspire towards. Also, she is certainly a beauty, although it is such a shame that you will never be able to appreciate it."

Stuart heard Alexa's footsteps coming down the hall. He stood up and moved closer to the open door. Alexa then ran straight in and threw her arms around him. "Oh Stuart, I have missed you terribly," she said, as she kissed his mouth. "These past two days, I have done nothing but think of you, and of that night you held me so close while we danced."

The Duke, who assumed that Alexa had not noticed his presence in the room, cleared his throat and said, "I am certainly surprised by your conduct Lady Alexa."

Alexa quickly jumped back from Stuart. She then stood with her head down looking ashamed and embarrassed. "Y…Your Grace, I did not know you were there," she quietly muttered.

The Duke moved close to Alexa. "Obviously, you did not. Do your parents know where you are?" he asked sternly.

"No," replied Alexa, looking up at the Duke like a naughty child. "They do not know. Please Your Grace, do not tell them! They would be so disappointed in me if they knew that I was secretly meeting a man, and with no one to chaperone. They will also be displeased to learn that I have lied to them. I told them I was going to spend the day with Lady Beatrice Wigglesworth, because my mother knew that she would be in need of company with her husband away in France for several days. But please, do not blame Stuart. He did not know that I had lied to them. The deception is mine alone."

It was true that Lady Beatrice would be alone for several days. Stuart had learned this through his business dealings two weeks earlier. He also knew that the Duke would welcome this bit of news. He would certainly not be able to resist paying her a visit that very day. Lady Beatrice's copious cleavage had always been one of his greatest weaknesses.

The Duke grinned at them both and then said, "Although my head tells me that my duty is to Lord and Lady Spence, I certainly do not have the heart to deny young love. Just this once, you may continue with your tryst, and I will not be informing your parents, Lady Alexa. And as for you Stuart, I trust that if I allow you to be alone with this lovely young woman, you will behave as a complete gentleman and at no time give in to your baser nature." The Duke chuckled.

"Oh thank you so much, Your Grace," Alexa said, smiling in flirtatious innocence. "You are too kind."

"And that, my dear girl, has always been my greatest problem. I am most definitely too kind," said the Duke, running his hand down Alexa's hair. He then turned to Stuart and said, "I have some business to attend to this afternoon and will likely be out all day. For this reason, I will not see you again until you return from your trip. When you do, I will be expecting a report of success."

"What trip?" asked Alexa, sounding worried and disappointed.

Stuart took her hand in his and said, "I am sorry, Alexa, but I have business outside of London and must go away for a few days. I promise, however, that I will return, and when I do, there is something important I would like to discuss with your father."

"You need not worry Lady Alexa," interjected the Duke. "I guarantee that Stuart will certainly return to you. He is not the kind of man to ever be unfaithful with another woman."

Alexa ignored the Duke and said to Stuart, "Will you tell me what you wish to discuss with my father?" She tried to put on her best oh-goody-he's-going-to-ask-me-to-marry -him face.

Stuart charmingly laughed, "No, Alexa. For the time being, you will have to wait until I speak with your father."

The Duke was feeling very pleased by all he was hearing. He clapped his hands together and exclaimed, "Well now, I suppose I shall be off, and give you two some privacy. You have things to discuss and I have things to attend to."

Alexa moved over and linked her arm with Stuart's. She smiled at the Duke and said, "Thank you again, Your Grace. I am deeply indebted to you."

The Duke was delighted by what he had heard. Without another word, he simply grinned and left the room, closing the door after him.

After Alexa was sure the Duke was gone, she let go of Stuart's arm and asked, "What next?"

"Give him time to leave the grounds. From the window, we can see his car exiting the gates. After that, I just need to find those papers while you wait here. I will bring them back to the office to copy out. You can help me do that. When we have copied all of the information, then I will have to return the originals to the place where I found them. From there, we will just need to get out of here."

"Well, I'm all for that," said Alexa. "This is one creepy pad."

# 13

It was raining outside, and Rose was playing with her dolls in the living room. Julia was Cinderella. A tissue wrapped around her waist transformed her nurse's uniform into a beautiful white ball gown. Her other two dolls were the mean stepsisters. A small stuffed teddy bear with only one eye was the prince. After the prince tried the little white shoe on Julia's foot, she revealed her identity by putting on the other one. The story was now complete. They simply kissed and went off to live happily ever after.

Rose rested Julia and the one-eyed bear against a chair leg that was to be their new home together. "The end," she said, and then looked around for some other fun thing to do.

In the far corner of the room was a small wooden trunk. It was hidden under a white tablecloth and topped with a simple green vase. This was Grandma's trunk. Rose never knew her grandmother, as she died a year before Rose was born, but she had looked through the trunk on more than one occasion. Jeannie had always allowed this.

Rose went over to the trunk and removed the vase and cloth. The black paint on the top was old and faded, but the design was still visible. It looked like two 'X's' side by side connected by a horizontal line through the center. She slowly opened the lid and breathed in the sweet smell of cedar. This was a smell that always made her feel instantly calm and happy.

Reaching inside, she was careful to take out the two delicate teacups that were on top. She set them gently on the floor beside her. They both had some small chips and the glaze was yellow and cracked. Each had a red rose painted on the inside. Rose touched one of the little flowers. *Rose, just like me*, she thought, as she did each time she removed them from the trunk.

Looking back inside, she then took out five different pieces of white linen which she piled beside the teacups. Under these was an old, framed print of a castle. Rose picked it up and closely examined the picture. It was everything a castle should be, with a large doorway in the middle and two tall towers on either side. She tried to imagine what it would be like to go inside and search every room and every passageway, uncovering all of its secrets. What great fun that would be!

Rose then put the print down and reached in to take out the last of her grandmother's treasures. It was a very old Bible that was frayed on the edges. Both the front and back covers had separated and there were many loose pages. The entire thing was held together by only an old brown shoelace tied in a little bow.

Rose pulled the lace and undid the bow. She then removed the front cover. Carefully, she turned the very first page and revealed the words that were written on the inside. Although she had looked at this inscription many times before, she had never been able to read it. It was in cursive writing, and Rose could not recognize the letters. This time it was different. At the end of that school year, Mrs. Simpson had taught her class handwriting, so Rose now knew how to read cursive.

She sat in silent amazement. All those times before, she could only marvel at the mystery and wonder what could have been written there so long ago. But now, things had changed. There it was as clear as day. It was like magic! She knew exactly what those words said. Rose put her finger under each one and read them aloud:

*To my loving husband Jupiter*
*Together we are One*

* * *

Stuart left Alexa alone in his office while he headed up to the Duke's private rooms. All of the security personnel were on the main floor, and they would not think it unusual if they happened to see him going upstairs. His worry was more about being seen by one of the many servants, who were always busy in the upstairs rooms and hallways.

Stuart carefully peered around every corner as he made his way through the corridors. If anyone here should see him, his presence would certainly be reported to the Duke. Although he could come up with some excuse, Stuart did not want to create too many complications. It was important not only for his own safety, but also for the safety of his uncle, that the Duke should have no suspicions.

So far, luck seemed to be on his side as the upper floor appeared to be all but deserted. He came to the large black and gold double entry doors, and slowly turned one of the handles. Stealthily slipping into the room, he then quietly closed the door behind him. Even with the curtains open, allowing the daylight in through the large leaded-glass windows, the extravagantly decorated room still seemed dark and dingy. Stuart wanted only to find those papers, and then get out of there as quickly as possible.

He looked at the Duke's mahogany credenza. This was the most opulent piece of furniture in the room, and the one place where he knew the papers would have to be stored. He opened the cupboard doors and looked inside. There were shelves with many documents, but he could not see the envelope that he had delivered to the Duke. He began to shuffle through the various papers and folders.

After a few minutes of searching, Stuart was beginning to worry. Perhaps the Duke had hidden the papers elsewhere. He looked around the room, but could not think where they could possibly be. The longer he spent in that room, the greater his chances of being caught. He had to think quickly about where else the Duke might have hidden them.

At a complete loss for ideas and beginning to feel desperate, Stuart found himself saying a small prayer. *"Oh God please! I must find those papers,"* he simply whispered.

Almost immediately after uttering those words, he noticed something within the credenza that he had not noticed before. Just below the lowest shelf was a decorative strip of wood. Although it appeared to be an ordinary part of the desk, something about it did not seem quite right. Stuart ran his fingers along the wood and gently tapped it. He then applied pressure in the center, and heard a small click. The strip of wood fell open, revealing a secret hiding place. He could see right away that there inside was the envelope he had been looking for.

Stuart sighed in relief. He removed the envelope and was just about to close the drawer when he suddenly got the feeling that someone was watching him. He turned his head and saw the Duchess dressed in a robe and slippers, silently staring at him. For a moment, Stuart did not know what to do, but he quickly gathered his thoughts and said, "Good day Duchess. The Duke has asked me to review these documents for him."

The Duchess just continued to silently stare. Finally she said, "Stuart, the Duke does not allow anyone inside the cupboard. Even I am forbidden to open those doors."

"I…I realize that is usually the case, however, today is different. It is a matter of urgency, and he has asked me to retrieve these papers from his room."

"I do not believe you," she told him curtly.

At this point, Stuart just stood there unable to think what else to say. Doubt and anxiety descended like dark clouds. Was this now the end? Finally, he had a chance to do something truly worthwhile, and it was turning all wrong. How could he have been so foolish to think that he could do this? He had let his uncle down. He was no Robin Hood. He was still just the Duke's idiot dog.

"How long has it been since I have seen you?" the Duchess asked.

Stuart was surprised by this unexpected question. He thought about it and realized that it had been a long time. "I believe that it has been about a year, Duchess," he answered.

"And did you ever wonder where I was?" she asked. "Did anyone ever wonder where I was?"

Stuart realized that he had never thought too much about the Duchess at all. She had always seemed more like an apparition than a woman—something there, and yet, not really present at all. "The Duke did mention that you were suffering from an illness," answered Stuart. "I asked him to pass on my wishes for your speedy recovery." This was true.

"Did you, Stuart? Did you really send wishes for my recovery? He did not tell me this," she said, taking a small step forward. "He never brought me well-wishes from anyone."

Just then Stuart became aware of how old and tired the Duchess was looking, and he also noticed that she may have been crying. "I am sorry that my wishes were not conveyed to you," he said. "But please know now that I did send them."

The Duchess sighed and asked, "And did he tell you that I was unstable? Does he tell people that?"

"No Duchess, only that you were ill," Stuart replied.

"Well, he has certainly let me know, on many occasions, that I was unstable," said the Duchess, turning her head towards the window.

Stuart could see that she was in great pain, and felt sympathy towards her. It was common knowledge that the Duke married her only for her money and title. "I am truly sorry, Duchess," he said, hoping to make her feel better. "You deserve far better."

The Duchess looked at Stuart and nervously laughed. "Oh Stuart, if he knew you were here, he would not hesitate to have you killed. Where do you find such courage to defy him like this? I never suspected that you had it in you, and the Duke certainly does not suspect."

Stuart had given up trying to lie to this woman. He did not have it in his heart to add to the deception in her already difficult life. "I fully understand the danger," he admitted, "but I have no regrets for what I am doing. I do regret, however, not being truthful with you. That was disrespectful of me, and I apologize."

For a while, the Duchess simply stared silently at Stuart. She then said, "You will have to put those papers back."

Stuart looked at the envelope in his hand and began to consider what to do next. He had come so close. How could he just give up now?  Before he could decide on what to say, the Duchess added, "Yes, they must be returned, but only after you have read them, or copied them, or whatever you have to do with them. You know full well that you will have to put them back. The Duke cannot find them missing."

For a moment, Stuart was not sure if he heard correctly. "Are you saying that you will allow me to take these documents, and that you will keep it from the Duke?" he asked in astonishment.

"Yes," sighed the Duchess, "I suppose I am. You have inspired me today, Stuart, and it has been a very long time since I have felt inspired by anything. Despite all I know about what has transpired between you and my husband, I find that I want you to succeed."

Stuart looked at the floor in shame. He had no idea the Duchess knew.

The Duchess walked over and tenderly placed her hand on his cheek. She looked into his eyes and said, "It is alright Stuart. I realize that in many ways we are the same. This is why I want victory for you. Somehow, your victory will be mine also."

The Duchess then reached over and closed the secret drawer of the credenza. "When you return this envelope, do not come to this room again. It is too dangerous. The Duke rewards his servants well, if they spot something out of the ordinary. Instead, bring it to me. If anyone sees you, you are merely bringing me information that I requested on healing springs. I will replace the envelope myself. It is still not unusual for me to be seen in my husband's rooms."

Stuart looked at the Duchess. He could see that she was not looking as tired and defeated as before. There was new life in her eyes. "Thank you," he said. "I promise to do my best for both of us."

Once back in his office, Stuart and Alexa quickly copied out every word that was in the papers. When they were finished, Stuart headed upstairs again.  As he walked through the hall, he passed three servants on his way. Each one eyed him with suspicion.  He felt no worry. If the Duchess said that she would cover for him, he believed her.

Stuart stood in front of the Duchess' door. Out of the corner of his eye, he noticed a servant spying from far down the hall. The man could see him, but was too far away to hear anything. Stuart knocked and waited.

The Duchess opened the door. She was now fully dressed and her hair was up. Stuart handed her the envelope, and whispered, "We are being watched."

As the Duchess took the envelope from him, she smiled at him and said, "Yes. I am aware, and as I said before, I will be able to handle any questions put to me later on." She then looked him in the eye and said, "I do not know what this is about, nor do I care to know. But whatever it is, Stuart, and whatever you will do with the information you now possess, Godspeed to you."

Stuart took her hand and kissed it respectfully. When he looked again at her face, he could see that she had begun to cry. He wished that he could say something to help, but realized there was nothing more he could do. Without another word, the Duchess took a step backwards and closed the door. Stuart quickly turned and headed downstairs to his car where Alexa would be waiting with the copies.

# 14

Stuart sat at the table and watched impatiently while his uncle carefully read over the papers. This was the third time his uncle was reading through them, and the entire thing seemed to be taking forever. Stuart desperately wanted to know if the information there was as important as the Duke seemed to think it was. Even though he had read them himself, he couldn't make much sense out of any of it.

Finally, Marlon looked up at Stuart. His eyes were filling with tears. "Oh my son, you are a hero!" he exclaimed. "You have done such an important thing by bringing me this information. It all makes sense. I now understand why the Duke believes that I have the missing piece to the puzzle. You have made it all come together! Without your courage, I would still be in the dark. You are remarkable, Stuart!"

Stuart blushed. Praise was not something he was used to, and he was not sure how to respond. There was a moment of silence and then he simply asked, "I have read through the documents, but what does it all mean?"

Marlon smiled. "It means that we are very close to finding the one whom the Duke is searching for."

"You mean the golden child?" asked Stuart.

"Yes," answered Marlon, "But more than that. She will have all three Holy Marks. She is not just any child. She is the Golden Grail."

"But how will we know which golden child is the right one. The Duke said that there were several born in 1961? I have been searching extensively, and so far have come up with nothing," said Stuart, who still had some doubt in his heart, but wanted to follow through for his uncle's sake.

"Let me explain to you how it all fits together," said Marlon. He then held up the papers in his hand. "In these documents are hints which appear to connect to research I have been conducting. I am unsure whether it was the Duke's rumor mill or one of his better soothsayers that pointed him in my direction, but his suspicions are correct. I do have information that may be significant in the location of the Golden Grail."

Marlon set the papers down on the table and then reached over to the nearby bureau. Opening a drawer, he took out a very thick and messy looking file folder. He placed the folder on the table next to the papers. "You see Stuart, I have been working on my own genealogy for some time now," he said. "As you know, the Bloodline is usually very well documented, but there was a blank in mine. It had to do with my mother. You know of course that my mother was not the same woman as your father's mother."

"Yes," said Stuart. "My father did explain that to me."

"Well, my mother's female line was recorded back as far as my great great grandmother, and then the records just end. There was no documented evidence as to her mother, which I found very unorthodox considering the great lengths to which our family has gone to preserve these details. I have spent years searching for the missing piece of the puzzle and, for a long time, was able to find merely snippets of information that only teased my desire to know the truth. However, there are things I have found of late that have now unraveled the mystery. "

Stuart was beginning to think more deeply about all his uncle was telling him. Could this truly be real? Was there actually a child who was the Golden Grail? For centuries, men had dreamed of this. They have hidden this dream in stories and songs. They have painted it in masterpieces. Some men have killed, and others have been killed in their quest for this one precious gift from God. Stuart knew he should be feeling afraid. If it was real, then this was something monumental. Only two weeks ago, such a thing would have been overwhelming for him, but not today. Instead, he was feeling exhilarated. For the first time in his life, he was beginning to understand the expression "*a taste of freedom.*"

Stuart waited for his uncle to continue the story, but was surprised when he divulged nothing further about what he had found. Instead, Marlon simply gathered up the papers and asked, "Have you ever been to America, my son?"

"No, Uncle. I have never been before," said Stuart who was, at first, confused by the question. "Does this now mean what I believe it means?"

Marlon reached over and patted Stuart on the shoulder. "Go home and pack your bags. Tell the Duke only that I have offered to take you to America—just a pleasant vacation to get to know you better. Assure him that you will watch me closely and immediately report anything suspicious. You must keep him believing in your loyalty."

Stuart was feeling excited by how fast things were moving. "How…how long will we be away?" he asked.

"I should not think more than two weeks, if all goes well. You understand that we are headed further into danger? We may not come out alive, my son. Before you leave to get your things, I feel that I must ask you once again. Are you certain that you wish to be involved?"

Stuart had previously thought about what this would mean. Because of Jack, he had thought very hard about the real possibility that it may not end well. But something deep inside told him that this was important. There were crucial things to be done, and he could not help feeling that he was the only one on the face of the earth who could do them. It was his destiny.

"Am I not Robin Hood?" he chimed to his uncle.

Marlon laughed. "Look at these priceless documents," he said, holding up the papers. "I would never have known about any of this, if it were not for you. You are indeed Sir Robin Hood."

* * *

Rose sat on the floor with Julia opposite her. She was the teacher and Julia was her pupil. "Now class, I will read you a story so please pay attention," said Rose in her most grown-up voice. She opened the cover of the old book in her hand and began to read:

*Once upon a time there was a Prince who wanted to marry a real princess. He searched the land, and met many who claimed to be a real princess. However, each princess he met along the way had something not quite right with her, which told him that this was not a real princess at all. Unable to find a real princess, the prince returned home sad and downtrodden.*

*One stormy night there was a knock on the castle door. When the Prince opened the door, he saw a woman, who was soaked by the rain. "I am seeking shelter," she said.*

*"Then please enter," said the Prince. The Prince was confused because in his heart he felt that this woman was a princess however, because her clothes were wet and muddy, she did not look at all like a princess should.*

*He whispered to his mother, "I believe that she is a princess, but how are we to know?"*

*His mother replied, "I shall put her to the test."*

*The Prince's mother then went and put down a tiny pea on the bed where the woman would sleep. She then piled twenty feather beds and twenty mattresses on top of the pea. "If she can feel the pea, then we will know for certain that she is a real princess," said the mother.*

*The next morning the Prince's mother asked the woman how she had slept. The woman replied, "Horribly! There was something very hard in that bed and I could not get a moment's rest. I am now black and blue all over."*

95

*The Prince and his mother were joyful that they had at last found a real princess. The Prince married her and they lived happily ever after.*
*The End*

Rose closed the book, and looked at Julia. "Did you like that ending?

Julia only answered with her small smile.

Rose suddenly had an idea! "We should try the test to see if we are princesses," she said to her doll.

Rose then ran out to the garden and pulled a pea pod from one of the plants. She smashed one end with a rock and then pried the pod open. Rose took out a single small green pea and ran back into the house.

"I have it," she said triumphantly to Julia, who was left sitting on the living room floor. Rose looked around the room and thought about how she could make a big bed. She didn't have twenty mattresses, and she did not even know what feather beds were. She considered her own mattress, but the springs were wearing through in the middle, so she would not be able to tell whether it was the pea or a bumpy spring.

Rose looked at the sofa. It had three fat cushions for the seat. She set the pea down on the wooden floor, then removed the three cushions and piled them one at a time on top. For a moment, she just stood back and looked at the little stack. Should she add more? She then took a thick folded blue blanket from the chair and placed it like a blue crown on the top of her small tower.

Rose stared at what she had built. It seemed stable enough to hold her. Although it was not twenty mattresses and twenty feather beds, she was, after all, only a little girl. A little girl should only need a little bed. The test should still work.

Rose carefully climbed up on top of the pile. It wobbled a little, but she was able to keep it balanced while she slowly positioned herself. Now lying on her back, she looked up at the cracks in the ceiling plaster, and tried to decide what she was feeling. It was not exactly clear. She then closed her eyes and concentrated very hard. At first, the pillows and blankets just seemed to make for a very soft bed, and she began to doubt. But just as she was ready to give up, she felt something strange. There in the middle of her back was something small, round and very uncomfortable. She could feel it! She could feel that tiny pea underneath all of those pillows!

Rose excitedly jumped up, and her little tower of pillows tumbled down. She quickly grabbed up Julia and ran to the kitchen where she knew her mother would be. As she bounded in, she could see her mother busy at the sink. "Mama! Mama!" she shouted, "I did the test!"

Jeannie put down the pot she was scrubbing and looked at her daughter. "I did the test!" repeated Rose.

"What test?" asked Jeannie.

"The princess test, and I passed!"

Jeannie was very confused, "What princess test?"

"You know," replied Rose, "from the story, *The Princess and the Pea*. I put down a pea and then lots of pillows, and I felt it! I felt the pea right here in my back!" Rose pointed to the center of her spine. "That means I'm a real princess!"

Jeannie smiled. "I guess it does," she said, and then went back to cleaning the pot.

Rose was immediately downhearted. It was obvious that her mother did not believe her. She looked sadly at Jeannie, who continued to busily scrub away. More than anything, Rose wished that her mother could understand, but she knew it was not possible. There was nothing she could say that would help her mother see the truth.

Rose clutched Julia tightly and quietly slipped out of the back door. Once outside, she went over to the big boulder and sat down beside it. She place Julia in front of her and looked at her pretty face. At least Julia understood. "Julia," she said, "you and I are the only ones who know. We are the only ones in this whole wide world who know that I am a real princess. I wish Mama could believe too."

Julia's gaze remained steadfast and her hint of a smile reminded Rose that, no matter how she was feeling now, in the end it would all be okay.

# 15

Stuart sat in the widow seat next to his uncle. He looked down at the sea that was so far below their plane. Although he had flown many times before, he felt as if this were his first time soaring through the air. There was a sense of invigoration as the plane flew over a cloud and he marveled at just how high off the earth he was.

"America is a very unusual place," said Marlon. "There are many different factions and sects within the family. Some of them are more than a little strange."

"What could be stranger than the Duke and his occult ceremonies?" asked Stuart.

Marlon thought about it. "Well, when you put it that way, I suppose nothing," he answered.

"I can understand why you called it a big bloody mess," said Stuart. "With all the political and religious divisions, it cannot be said to be anything else. I have had to deal with several of these groups over the phone, and it was not an easy task to try and communicate with them."

Marlon moved his seat into a reclining position and said, "It is not the divisions that make it a mess. That is just another symptom of the disease. It is the big lie—the lie that those in the Bloodline have God-given rights on this earth—rights that those outside the group do not. Sometimes it makes me sick to think of all of the wars and suffering they have caused in this world— all because of this false belief that they are smarter, stronger and better than other human beings. With this foolish and vain belief, not only do they hurt others, but they also cause themselves and their children a great deal of unnecessary pain. It is a horrible way to exist—always trying to live up to some ridiculous imaginary god-man, and inevitably always falling to the level of grubbing swine. In such an existence, there is little room for love, or family, or anything else that makes life worth living. It is dysfunction at its best.”

This was a very new perspective for Stuart. He was well aware of the suffering caused to others throughout history, but he had never really considered that there was also intense suffering within the Bloodline itself. Stuart remembered his father who smiled and laughed with practiced charm in social situations, but who never seemed to smile or laugh in private. In private he was always stern, reserved and seemed very unhappy. Stuart had never before considered that his father lived a life of suffering, but he saw it now.

“To tell you just how truly messed up it all is,” said Marlon, “there are several groups, who actually believe that they are not human at all. They have convinced themselves that they are genetically superior space aliens, who are just waiting for the mother ship to come and get them. Some days I wish that there really was a mother ship to take them away. Fools! Absolute fools!”

“If I had my way,” continued Marlon, “I would write a book and tell the whole world the truth. But really, who would have the courage to publish such a thing, and would people be able to believe it?”

As he considered all that his uncle had said, Stuart began to fill with doubt about everything. If the ideas behind the Bloodline were fictional, why was he now crossing the ocean in quest of the Golden Grail? He looked at his uncle and asked, “If it is all just a false construct, why then are we pursuing this prophecy? If it is all just a lie, then why are we flying all the way to America, and risking our lives to follow a mere fantasy?”

Marlon smiled, and patted Stuart’s arm. “Oh, that is a very good question,” he said. “We are on this quest because this is not part of the fantasy. What we follow is not about the imagined world of men who create gods in their own image.

This is about the real world of God. This part is no fabrication. God is very real. God is, in fact, the only reality. Whatever all of this truly means, it is something so mysterious that it is beyond our comprehension. I may not understand it completely, but what I know for certain is that it is not about the superiority of one human being over another, or creating a superhuman. It is not about domination and oppression. I know that it has everything to do with the expression of God's love for every single man, woman and child. It has to do with the fulfillment of God's loving promise to us all."

Marlon went silent and closed his eyes. Stuart sat and waited to hear more. A couple of minutes passed and he began to wonder if his uncle had fallen asleep. All of a sudden Marlon opened his mouth and said, "Whatever you do, my son, never underestimate God. Question everything man-made and man-said, but never underestimate God. If you have days where you cannot distinguish between that which is God and that which is man, then remember—even though man carries a resemblance to God, God looks nothing at all like man. Now, if you do not mind, I believe I need a nap. It is a very long flight, and I am not young anymore."

Stuart turned back to look out at the clouds below. Marlon's words were not easy to comprehend, but he found that he was starting to understand. As he continued to gaze out the window, the sight of the beautiful sky just seemed to confirm all his uncle had said. The entire thing was beginning to seem so real. Maybe a Divine promise was being fulfilled. Maybe his uncle was right.

Suddenly, a tremendous emotion rose up in Stuart. He could hear his heart pumping and feel the hot living blood course through his veins. His body was alive and electric. Stuart had felt this way before, but it was a very long time ago. He had forgotten about it, and only now did the memory come back to him. Every summer, when he was home from school, he experienced this very feeling. From the top of the lane, he would ride his bicycle at full speed straight down the steep hill. This was the same feeling. It felt just as if he were soaring with absolute freedom towards something inexplicably wonderful!

The sun had set long ago, as Rose sat perched on the boulder in her backyard. She sometimes liked to come out here after it was dark. Jeannie allowed this as long as she stayed within the yard. Rose wasn't afraid of the dark, especially now that she had Julia to sit with her. Besides which, with the moon and the stars, there really was no such thing as darkness. It was just a different kind of light.

The moon was shining brightly, and the sky was ripe with stars. Rose looked up and searched for the Big and Little Dippers. In the winter, she had learned about these two constellations from a schoolbook. She knew that by finding one of the brightest stars, she would find the Little Dipper. From there, it was easy to find the Big Dipper, which was always close by.

Rose was happy when she easily found both of them. She then looked around in amazement at all of the other stars. "Do you wonder what they are?" she asked Julia. "You know, like in the song *Twinkle Twinkle Little Star*. In the book I read, it said that they are fireballs, like the sun. Isn't it funny that fireballs do look like diamonds when they are far away?"

Rose then looked to the south and saw a light moving slowly across the sky. When she was younger, she thought that this meant that a star had come alive, and had decided to travel the universe. It seemed likely because something similar did happen in the story *A Little Lost Star*. But when she told her mother about it, Jeannie explained that the moving star was in fact an airplane. It looked like a small point of light because it was just so far away. Rose had not been disappointed to learn the truth. It still seemed amazing that those little specks of light were flying ships full of people sailing through the night sky. The truth was just as magical, if not more so.

As she watched the plane move slowly across the starry sky, Rose was shocked to see a sudden and unexpected streak of light. It moved so fast that she would have missed it if she had been looking the other way. Although she had never seen anything like it before, she knew immediately what it was. It was a falling star!

Rose was filled with excitement. She knew what this meant. This meant that she got a wish! A wish on a falling star must be the best kind of wish there was. It would be much more powerful than a birthday candle wish. Birthday candles came every year, but a falling star was something special. She closed her eyes and thought hard about what she would wish for.

There were many things she would like. There were wonderful toys she had seen on television commercials, or nice new clothes. Rose could not make up her mind. Somehow those things seemed too small for a falling star wish. No…this wish had to be the biggest ever. Rose realized that she needed time. As far as she knew, there were no rules about when a falling star wish had to be made. She would keep it, and when the time was right, she would know what to wish for.

* * *

Marlon put the key in the door and opened it. He let Stuart go in first, and then followed him. "Well, it is not the Royal Suite," he said, "but it will do. Which do you prefer, bed closest to the window, or closest to the lavatory?"

"Window please," said Stuart.

Marlon smiled. "Given my age, that is likely the wisest choice for both of us."

Stuart laughed and placed his suitcase on the luggage stand. "And exactly how much should I be unpacking?"

"Not too many items," answered Marlon. "I am unsure just how long we will be staying. It could be several days, or we may have to leave tomorrow. It all depends on what information my contact can provide. I will be going alone to meet up with her tomorrow morning."

Stuart was feeling a little hurt that he was not being included in this meeting. His uncle's opinion had become important to him, and he wanted to be sure that Marlon did not doubt his loyalty. "I know that as I tried to deceive you once, you would definitely be within your rights to be suspicious. But please believe me when I say that everything is different now. I am completely devoted to your mission," said Stuart, hoping that his uncle would know that he was being sincere.

Marlon looked at him and smiled. He could see how much Stuart needed his reassurance. "Here in New York," he said, "there are places where I must go alone. It is not that I do not trust you, Stuart. It is all about the security system that is in place, and how we in the Underground pass on information. Once you are fully cleared and officially join us, if of course that is what you choose, then you may learn more of how things are done, and you will be able to attend any meeting. But for now, the protocol for this particular city is that I must go alone."

Stuart was relieved that his uncle did trust him, but disappointed that he would not be more fully involved. He felt like he wanted to join the Underground immediately. He wanted to be a part of the secret work that they did. But at the same time, he fully understood the precaution. "Just let me know how I may be of help. I am up for it, Uncle Marlon. I promise that I will do whatever is needed."

Marlon placed his suitcase on the other luggage rack and said, "I hope you will be ready to fulfill that promise. I am certain that the time will come when I will very much need your help."

Stuart felt heartened by his uncle's confidence in him. He was certain that he would be ready whenever that time came.

As he unzipped his suitcase, Stuart suddenly recalled something he had uncovered while working for the Duke. It was something that could possibly be significant. "Uncle," he said, "About this child we are looking for—well, I believe that I might know who she is. You see, there is one whom I found living not far from New York—a golden child born in 1961, but the Duke, without any explanation, simply dismissed her. Could he have passed over the one we are looking for?"

"No, that is not the one," Marlon bluntly replied, as he began to unpack a few items.

Stuart was surprised by how quickly his uncle pushed the suggestion aside. "How can we know for certain?" he asked.

"Because, I know of her" said Marlon. "And firstly, she does not have the Grail. That is a fact. And secondly, she is not truly Golden."

Stuart was confused. "But her photo? I saw her photo."

"Yes," said Marlon. "But that child was not born with that ratio. The parents in their ambition had a surgeon change her face to appear golden."

"They did that to a child?" Stuart exclaimed.

"Never underestimate the cruel ambition of some people," Marlon told him.

Stuart was silent as he thought about it.

Marlon then walked over and sat down on his bed. "Sit down, my son," he said. "I want to explain something to you."

Stuart sat down on his own bed across from his uncle.

Marlon looked seriously at his nephew. Stuart could see that what he was going to say was important. "I am now going to tell you why the Duke believed that I had the information he needed," said Marlon. "It is all about the historical and genealogical research I have been conducting. It has taken me years to piece together the story, but I believe that I have finally found the truth. Although there are no official records to support it, I am certain that this tale is what actually transpired.

"It began here in America at the very end of the Revolution. A woman of The Vine, who was in fact a sister to one of the Duke's ancestors, was banished to live in the American wilderness. While here, she fell in love with a slave. The slave was African on his mother's side and of the Bloodline on his father's. They ran off together and were able to live for a few years in peace. Eventually, they were found out, and rather than be separated and give up their secret, they jumped together into the Niagara River. Their secret was of two daughters, both of whom possessed the Grail. Several years passed before a Bloodline group in Scotland caught wind of a rumor about the girls. An investigator was sent to America, and he did in fact discover that it was true. There were two girls, and each did have the Grail Mark. There was concern about the fact that the girls had some recognizable African features which would not easily be accepted among many within the Bloodline, so a choice was made. They took the younger girl who would be able to pass as a woman of French or Spanish nobility, and they left the older one whose more African features would definitely give both herself and her sister away.

"The younger girl who was brought to England was eventually married to a man within the Bloodline. This woman was in fact my great great grandmother. The older girl was left behind. She is the key to our quest. We must now find the scattered pieces of information that will help follow her genealogical trail to the present day. I believe that this trail will lead us to the child we seek." Marlon paused, looked at Stuart, and waited for his reaction.

At first, Stuart did not know what to think of this story. He looked at his ring and said, "Do you mean to tell me that this child is from a lost branch of the Vine?" He had never imagined that such a thing could happen. The Bloodline was so careful to always keep their own well-identified.

Marlon leaned forward. His voice was suddenly filled with passion. "Do you not see, my son," he said. "What we are doing here in New York is work of the highest order. This is something so amazing that it is difficult to completely comprehend. This is a crucial puzzle piece that makes sense of everything that ever was in this world. We are searching for *the branch from the stump of Jesse. We are searching for *the stone which the builders rejected, but will become the corner stone.* We are searching for the fulfillment of God's greatest promise—the key to the ultimate salvation of humankind!"

Stuart felt the hairs stand up on the back of his neck, as strange chills ran through his body. This was no joke. This was real. His reasoning suddenly became cloudy, and he was filled with a single indescribable urge. It was an urge that moved beyond mere desire and into desperate necessity. Stuart was overcome with the intense hunger to find the Golden Grail.

# 16

The next morning, as Marlon was about to go and meet with his contact, he told Stuart not to leave the hotel. "I am still not entirely certain about the security in this city," he said. "So for your own safety, I suggest that you remain here. This may be an unnecessary precaution, but for now, I think that it is best."

Stuart was disappointed that he would not be able to take in some of the sights. It seemed such a shame to come all this way just to remain stuck inside of a hotel room. However, he resigned himself to following his uncle's instruction.

By late afternoon, Stuart was extremely bored and sick of watching American television. He went to the window and looked out at the vibrant busy city below. It seemed so full of life and people, and all he wanted was to go down there and mix in with the crowd. He was beginning to feel extremely frustrated and knew that he would have to do something soon.

He thought about ordering room service, but then had a better idea. Marlon asked him not to leave the hotel, but he did not say anything about leaving the room. Surely it could not hurt if he went down to the bar to have a drink or two. If he stayed in that room alone any longer, he felt like he would go completely mad. What harm could there be in just going downstairs?

Stuart freshened up and put on a nice suit. He thought that he might as well dress-up a little, especially if this was all he might experience of New York City. Before he went out the door, he left a note on the hotel notepad telling Marlon where he would be.

When Stuart arrived at the lounge, it was nearly empty. There were two attractive well-dressed women at a table near the door, and over at the far wall were three men who appeared to be having a business meeting. Stuart walked over to the curved bar and took a seat at the end. From here, he had a view of the entrance, in case his uncle returned looking for him.

Stuart ordered a gin and tonic. Jack always kidded him about this drink of choice. He referred to it as "an old lady's drink" and would dare Stuart to "swig pints like a man." Jack would joke that when they went to Liverpool, if Stuart ever ordered a gin and tonic in the pub, he would have to sit at a different table. Stuart would pretend to be offended, but they both knew that he thought it funny too.

Still feeling a little lonely and bored, Stuart drank his first drink too quickly. Almost immediately, it made him feel better. He then ordered a second glass, this time a double. As he began to drink this one back almost as fast, he started to yearn for some conversation. He looked over at the bartender, but the man was now busy at the other end of the bar pouring new orders for the businessmen.

Stuart glanced in the direction of the table with the ladies. He could see them looking at him and smiling. They then whispered and laughed to each other. It was obvious that they thought him attractive, and were hoping that he would come over. Stuart considered going over there just to have a little company.

He took another sip of his drink, and then looked at the ladies again. This time they were not looking at him. This time they stared in the direction of the entrance. Stuart then looked over too, and in the doorway was a tall and very handsome man dressed in the whitest suit he had ever seen. The man wore a commanding white Stetson on his head, which made him seem even taller, and under his jacket, a contrasting black t-shirt stretched across his wide chest. His pointy toed cowboy boots were shiny black and white, and clicked against the tile floor as he walked. The man sauntered towards the bar. As he passed by the ladies, he smiled and tipped his hat, making them both blush.

He sat down at the bar not far from Stuart, then removed his hat and shook out his corn silk hair. "Barkeep," he exclaimed in a rich Texas accent, "double scotch straight-up, no ice!" The bartender poured him the drink. He took a large gulp and then looked over at Stuart.

Stuart looked away, hoping that the man did not think he was staring.

"Looks like you're runnin' dry partner," said the man.

"Pardon me?" said Stuart confused.

The man laughed a deep smooth laugh. "Your drink buddy," he said pointing at Stuart's almost empty glass. "Can I buy you another?"

Stuart felt a little embarrassed that he had not understood the first time. "Oh my drink, yes of course. Uh? Yes, I suppose I could use another."

The cowboy snapped his fingers and said, "Barkeep, hit my friend again." He then got up and moved over beside Stuart. He put out his hand and said, "The name is Walker, and you are?"

Stuart shook the cowboy's hand noticing the firm and weighty handshake. "I am Stuart," he answered.

"Howdy Stuart. Judgin' from the way you talk, you're a long ways from home."

Stuart took a drink from the fresh gin and tonic now in front of him. "Yes, I suppose I am. I am from London."

"Never been to London myself," said Walker.

In his mind, Stuart laughed as he imagined this man, in his flashy white ensemble, walking down the streets of London. He then realized that he was beginning to get a little drunk.

"It's hot in here ain't it," said Walker, removing his suit jacket and fully revealing the very tight black t-shirt he wore. Stuart couldn't help but notice his large muscular arms. There was an ace of clubs tattooed on one of his biceps.

"I'm up here on business, Stuart. You here on business too?"

"No," answered Stuart. "Actually, I am vacationing with my uncle."

"Well, ain't that nice," replied Walker, who then took another sip of the scotch. "You definitely picked the finest hotel in New York. When I come up this way, I always stay here in the Presidential Suite. It's a real grand old place to be. I got myself a king-sized bed, complimentary champagne and all the caviar you can eat." The cowboy then leaned over to Stuart and said in his ear, "But to tell you the truth, I ain't a caviar sort of guy."

Stuart looked straight ahead and quickly took another long drink. Could this man be making a pass at him?

"You know Stuart, I'm a bettin' man, and I bet that you and me could be very good friends. Why not come on upstairs and see for yourself how nice the Presidential Suite is?"

Stuart felt for a moment like time had stopped. This man was coming on to him! This man, who was perhaps the most handsome he had ever seen in his life. Stuart's head was spinning. The gin and tonics were clouding his mind. He thought about the Presidential Suite. He thought about being in the exciting city of New York so far from home. He thought about this gorgeous man next to him. It would be so easy to just forget everything, get into the elevator and go straight up to the top floor.

Stuart turned his head and almost looked into Walker's steel-blue eyes, but instead he glanced past him and at the bartender who was busy cleaning glasses at the other end of the bar. It was then that the bartender reached up and switched on the radio. The Hollies were singing their latest hit. Stuart began to laugh as the sound of Jack's favorite group filled the room.

The cowboy was confused. "What's so funny?" he asked, trying not to show his annoyance.

Stuart, still laughing, said, "Oh, it is not you. It is something else entirely. I am so sorry, but I must turn down your offer."

Walker seemed very surprised. He stood up, put on his hat, and picked up the jacket beside him. Before he left, he leaned into Stuart's ear and said, "If you change your mind partner, you know where I am."

Stuart sat for a moment listening to the music and feeling so grateful that it was playing. Suddenly, he felt a hand on his shoulder and thought that the cowboy had returned. He turned around ready to rebuff the man once more when he found himself looking into his uncle's face.

"How many have you had?" Marlon asked. He could see that Stuart was a little drunk.

"It is only my third," he replied.

"Well I suppose that is not too serious then. You will still be able to leave in a few hours."

"Are we to leave already? We just got here." Stuart was now feeling like he really needed a good night's sleep.

"We must leave, and we must do it in the middle of the night," said Marlon.

"Why in the middle of the night?" asked Stuart.

"Because I saw one of the Duke's men in the lobby just now. We have been followed."

Stuart was surprised. "Is he someone you know?"

"No, I have never seen the man before."

"Then how could you be sure he works for the Duke?" asked Stuart.

"Because of the ace of clubs tattooed on his arm," his uncle replied.

Rose sat in the bed of periwinkle with her doll beside her. She watched as a honeybee moved from flower to flower sipping out the nectar. Popping one off of the stem, she then put her tongue to the little purple flower. She could taste the tiny drop of sweet nectar that was hidden there. Looking at the little bee working so hard, Rose said to Julia, "That bee is right. There is good stuff in those flowers."

Rose saw Lizzy walking towards her. Her hand was full of raspberries and the juice dripped red from her fingers. She was quickly devouring them.

"Where did you get those berries?" asked Rose.

With her mouth full of berries, Lizzy curtly replied, "My mother bought them."

Rose knew she was lying. She knew that Lizzy had been stealing them from Jeannie's raspberry patch. Despite Lizzy having a good house and good clothes, she would not hesitate to steal anything belonging to Rose and her mother. The first time Rose knew that Lizzy was a thief was when she stole the white feather. Rose had found the feather in her favorite tree, and decided that it was a magical feather. She had shown it to Lizzy and then stuck it in the ground near the boulder while she went in for lunch. When she returned, it was gone. Later that day she saw it in Lizzy's hand and asked for it back. Lizzy merely replied, "Finders keepers, losers weepers."

Unfortunately, there was no recourse for Rose. She tried to tell her mother about Lizzy when the feather was stolen, but Jeannie quickly dismissed the matter. Jeannie was simply not able to confront Lizzy's mother with her fancy hair-do and fashionable house dress. Rose quickly realized that Jeannie was powerless, and that meant so was she.

Despite the way things were, Rose always felt in her heart that there was real justice somewhere. There was a real good and a real bad. God and Jesus knew it, the honeybee knew it, the feather knew it, Julia knew it, and even the boulder knew it. Why Lizzy and so many other people could not see it, she did not know. They made up their own good and bad. For them, good was the thing they wanted and bad was not getting it.

"Go away" said Rose. "I don't like you."

Lizzy just laughed and pretended not to be bothered. As she walked by Rose, she said, "I'm having a birthday party next week with a real magician, and you're not invited."

For a moment, Rose wished that she could see a real magician. She had only seen them on television, and wondered what a real live one would be like. But then she thought carefully about it, and realized that a magician is not something she would want to see at all. She yelled after Lizzy, "He's a phony! He doesn't do real magic! It's just a trick he plays on you!"

Lizzy turned, stuck out her tongue and then ran off.

Rose looked at Julia. "She pretends that what I say doesn't matter, but she knows I'm right. That's why she's running."

# 17

About four hours had passed since Marlon and Stuart had left the darkened city in their rented sedan. The combination of the long over-seas flight and the gin and tonics had finally gotten the better of Stuart, who had fallen into a deep dreamless sleep in the passenger seat. He was surprised when he awoke to find the sun shining in his face. Wiping his eyes, he then stared at the road ahead, and tried to imagine where they could possibly be.

Marlon glanced at him and smiled. "Good, you're awake. We will be stopping to rest very shortly."

Stuart's head was hurting a little. "I have no argument against more rest," he said, as he stretched out his arms and legs a little.

As they continued to drive, there was not much more than trees and fields on either side of the road. Suddenly in the distance, they saw what appeared to be a large colorful neon sign. As they got closer, they could see that it was a tall smiling man dressed in green with a full quiver strapped to his back and a bow in his hand. The words on the sign said: *Robin Hood Motel.* There was also the word *Vacancy* in big red letters underneath.

"Well, what could be more perfect?" said Marlon.

"Indeed," laughed Stuart.

They pulled into the parking lot, and got out of the car. The motel was very modern and had the fresh look of being newly built. It was surrounded by a beautiful tall forest. Stuart silently laughed to himself as he wondered if this could be Sherwood Forest.

"You get the luggage from the boot, and I'll get us a room," said Marlon, who then headed for the door marked *Office*.

Stuart removed the bags and waited beside the car for his uncle. It was not long before Marlon came out again. He waved a key in the air and said "Lucky number 7! This must certainly be a good sign."

When they entered the room, they could see that it was cheerfully bright and decorated in fashionable primary colors. Marlon kicked off his shoes, pulled back the bed cover on the closest bed, and lay down. "I am too tired to change," he mumbled. "I'll just sleep in these clothes."

Stuart wasn't feeling much better. He lay down on the other bed, looked at the ceiling and wished that the dull pain in his head would soon stop. "Uncle," he said, "where are we going?"

"To Canada," Marlon replied sleepily.

Stuart was surprised to hear that they were leaving the United States. He had never imagined their quest would lead them to Canada. "And how do we know that the Duke's men are not following us?" asked Stuart.

"I have faith that we have escaped them," replied Marlon.

Stuart found Marlon's confidence surprisingly reassuring. He looked up at the white ceiling and began to think about something that had been on his mind for a while. It was something that he wanted to mention before, but felt too uncomfortable to raise the issue. "Uncle," he said.

"Yes, what is it now?" asked Marlon, wishing only that Stuart would be quiet so that he could sleep.

"I should have told you this before, and I know that this may not be the best time to address it, but when the Duke gave me the assignment, he also mentioned that you were being assessed. Do you know what that means?" Stuart had a good idea what it meant and was hoping he would not have to say the words aloud.

"Yes, Stuart. It means they were determining whether or not I pose a sufficient risk for termination."

"I am worried for you," said Stuart.

"They may kill me. They may not kill me. It is no matter. My only concern now is to find the Golden Grail."

"Well, they have let you go on this long. Perhaps in the end, they will not bother," said Stuart hopefully.

Marlon opened his eyes and turned his head towards Stuart. "Would you like to know why the Duke has not yet killed me? There is a reason why I have lived this long. It is the same reason your father blamed me for failing to restore our family to its original social stature. It is something I possess, and something that he always felt he deserved."

Stuart was surprised that the conversation had suddenly turned to his father. "What do you mean?" he asked his uncle.

"You can see for yourself," said Marlon. "Come here and touch the crown of my head."

For a moment, Stuart was in shock. It could not be! He had heard of it, but it was still just a myth in his mind. Could it be the Holiest of Marks? Why else would Marlon tell him to touch the crown of his head? Was it really the Grail? He stood up and took a step over to Marlon who remained lying on the bed. Stuart reached down and felt through the coarse grey hair. There was a small bowl-like area in his uncle's skull. It was real! Uncle Marlon possessed the Holy Grail! Stuart did not know what to say.

"That is why your father was so angry. Do you realize that with this pathetic little dandruff collector I could have been anything. I could even have been Prime Minister. He never forgave me for turning my back on all of it. This, too, is why the Duke has allowed me to go on so long. So far, he is too afraid to kill me, but that may change."

Stuart sat back down on his bed and looked in amazement at Marlon, who had now shut his eyes and was beginning to fall asleep. He stared at his uncle's unassuming grey hair that, all this time, had held the great secret. It was astonishing! Day by day everything was looking so different. Only weeks ago, Stuart was certain of the world as he knew it, but now all that was quickly fading away. *I was blind but now I see*, he thought to himself, as he marveled at everything he had never imagined but was there all along.

Stuart put his feet up on the bed and then gently laid his head on the pillow. Only then did he realize that his headache was completely gone. He closed his eyes thinking, *the truth is changing me—it is setting me free.*

* * *

When Stuart awoke from his deep sleep he was, at first, confused and disoriented. Sitting up, he looked around the room trying to remember where he was. It did not take long for it to come flooding back to him. *The Robin Hood Motel*, he chuckled to himself. *Where else would I be?*

He looked over at the dim light that came through a crack in the curtains and could see that it was now dusk. A table lamp on the desk in the far corner was switched on, providing some additional light in the room.

Stuart thought about the secret his uncle had revealed before they fell asleep. It was now very clear why his father had so deeply hated his own brother. The idea that anyone in the family would not take full advantage of such an incredible gift would be absolutely unthinkable to a man like him. He completely believed in taking whatever you could get in this world, and would often quote Ayn Rand, who he espoused as a great prophetess.

Glancing over to the other bed, Stuart saw that his uncle was no longer there. Instantly, he felt a wave of panic wash over him, but it quickly dissipated when he realized that the bathroom door was closed and he could hear the sound of running water. Knowing that Marlon had the Mark of the Grail was making Stuart feel even more protective about his uncle.

Stuart switched on a second lamp by the bed which brightened the room considerably. Hanging on the wall near the desk was a framed vintage movie poster. In the foreground of

116

the picture was a big red shield with the words, *The Adventures of Robin Hood*. Robin, with his trademark green hat and Mona Lisa-like smile, had his bow drawn, and an arrow aimed and ready to fire. Behind him, the raven haired Maid Marion looked on with mild trepidation. Stuart laughed a little at the idea that he could possibly live up to such an image. Still, he had to admit that he never felt more confident or full of courage than he did now.

It was not long before Stuart heard the water stop. A few moments later, Marlon came out of the bathroom showered, shaved and changed into clean clothing. He looked at his nephew and smiled. "A man of my age should be completely knackered after all that flying and driving, but I feel just full of energy. In fact, I feel younger than I have in years."

Stuart looked at his uncle's face, and said, "I would say that you do look younger." Suddenly worried that perhaps he was being rude, he then added, "Not that you ever looked that old, mind you."

Marlon laughed and patted Stuart on the back. "You do not have to try to explain. I will take it as a compliment." He then looked carefully at Stuart. "And I would have to say that you, my son, are looking older—but also in good way. One could explain it as a maturing of sorts."

"Thank you Uncle Marlon," said Stuart. "I do feel both older and wiser. And it is a very good feeling."

Stuart pointed over at the movie poster. "So, if I am to be Robin Hood, who then does that make you—Friar Tuck maybe?"

Marlon laughed. "Well, first off, I am not that fat. And secondly, Friar Tuck shaved the crown of his head in accordance with his order. I would not want to walk around with my crown exposed. Now would I?"

Stuart smiled. "I suppose that would not be wise."

Marlon began to pack up his things. "Now, if you would like to take your turn in the lavatory, we may then get something to eat at the restaurant. After that, we shall be off to our next destination."

Before Stuart went into the bathroom, he looked at his uncle and said. "I just want to thank you for trusting me enough to tell me about your Holy Mark."

Marlon shook his head. "It is supposed to be a great gift," he said. "However, in so many ways it has been more of a curse for me than anything else. There were so many expectations placed upon me as a young man. I was the family prize. Finally, I just could not take it anymore and I left. Your grandfather would have disowned me for that, if not for the fact that he always held out the hope that I would return. And if I thought that things would be different, I would have come back. But I always knew that no matter what nice words were said, I would still just be treated as an object to be possessed, and not loved as a son."

Stuart understood completely. "People will sacrifice anything for imagined power," he said, surprised to hear himself talk like that. This was usually the kind of thing Jack would say.

Marlon sighed and added, "The world is full of desperate sick men seeking to possess unique objects and gain what they believe is power in any way they can—sick men who will go so far as to want to control the entire world. It has been going on for far too long, and the fools continue to believe it is possible. What a stupid and naïve idea that the world can be simply harnessed and driven like a dumb beast. Do you know Stuart that someone had even came up with a formula for controlling the world? The Romans acquired it and used it for centuries in an attempt to control their own population, as well as the people they conquered. Such simple men never even consider that this is God's world and always will be. In their blind arrogance, they cannot even begin to imagine how insignificant their imagined conquests really are."

Stuart was surprised by what his uncle had just said. "There is a formula for world domination? That must be a carefully guarded secret," he remarked.

Marlon laughed. "Would you like to hear it my son?"

Stuart was shocked by such a cavalier response. "You know the formula? Of course I would want to hear it! Who wouldn't?" He waited intently to hear what his uncle had to say.

"All right," said Marlon. "Listen closely and I will tell you the secret formula for controlling humankind." He then paused and smiled slyly. Stuart was growing impatient and could see that his uncle was finding it amusing. Finally, Marlon opened his mouth and exclaimed, "*Now, Dasher! now, Dancer! now, Prancer and Vixen! On, Comet! on Cupid! on, Donder and Blitzen!*"

Stuart just stared at his uncle in confusion. This had to be a joke, but Marlon wasn't laughing. "Is…is that not from a children's poem about Father Christmas?" he asked.

"Yes it is Stuart," answered his uncle. "Some men believe that the best place to hide things is within plain view. Think about the names and consider the ways men attempt to build financial and political empires. But enough of that, we are wasting valuable time, so please go wash and dress. I don't know about you, but I am completely famished."

Stuart silently got up from the bed and headed to the bathroom where he would try to contemplate the strange thing he had just been told.

* * *

Rose sat on a rock near the river's edge. Her flip flops were beside her and her bare feet were in the shallow water. Julia sat nearby on a smaller rock.

"Hi Rose," a voice said behind her.

Rose turned and saw Pauly. Pauly lived just down the street from Rose. At one time, he would come over to play in her yard almost every day, but she rarely saw him anymore. Despite the fact that they always enjoyed each other's company, he stopped coming about two years prior. Ever since starting school, Pauly avoided Rose as much as possible. She knew that if he was talking to her now that he must be alone. Otherwise, he would not risk someone calling him an *Injun-lover*.

"Hi," said Rose, who was just glad to have someone around.

Pauly was dressed in his summer shorts and a t-shirt. He took off his shoes and socks and walked into the shallow water at the edge of the river. As he waded around, he stared down into the green tinted water and searched for gold. He had once seen some men on television find gold in a river, and always thought that it was just a matter of time before he was able to find gold too.

"Look a baby lobster," he said excitedly to Rose, forgetting for a moment about the gold.

"That's a crayfish Pauly," said Rose. "Lobsters live in the sea, not in a river." It was not unusual for Pauly to get confused about things.

Pauly didn't respond, but just kept walking around in the water that was now half-way up his calves. "There's lots of baby fish," he said. "I wish I had a net to catch them."

"You could use your shirt," suggested Rose.

Pauly looked with confusion down at this shirt. "That's silly," he said.

"Take off your shirt," said Rose. "Then put it on your arms, so that it stretches out flat in the middle. You can use it like a net and scoop up the fish." Rose held out her arms in position to give him a better idea of how to do it.

Pauly understood what Rose was telling him. She always had good ideas. He took off his shirt and put it on his arms just like she told him. He then looked down into the water, and spotted some minnows. Stabbing his arms fiercely below the surface, he tried to quickly gather them up. Pauly then stood just staring into the shirt. It did not take long before he realized that he had not caught even one. "It don't work," he said disappointedly.

"No Pauly," said Rose. "You have to put your net in the water and wait for the fish to swim into it. Then you carefully and slowly scoop them up. They have to trust you first. They have to know that you don't want to hurt them."

Pauly carefully followed Rose's instructions. He looked again into his t-shirt and marveled at what was there. Three tiny minnows were flipping and flopping around. "It worked," he shouted, smiling at Rose.

Rose smiled back. It felt good to be there with Pauly. It reminded her of a time when they used to have fun together. "Let them go now," she called out. "They need to get big."

Pauly tried it again and again. With each attempt, he was becoming more skilled, and catching more minnows. He moved slowly through the water focusing only on hunting for a new school of fish.

Rose wanted to stretch her legs a little. She grabbed Julia and stood up. Glancing over at Pauly, she became a little concerned when she realized that the water was now up to the bottom of his shorts. "Don't go out too far. It gets real deep all of a sudden," she called to him.

Pauly didn't acknowledge hearing her, and just kept trying to catch fish. He then spotted a school of some of the biggest fattest minnows he had ever seen, and began to move forward to get into position. Suddenly, his right foot plummeted into nothingness. He had reached the drop-off point. Pauly was instantly consumed by the dark water! The instinct to live rose up within him and he began to thrash his arms and legs wildly. In an instant, his head was once again in the open air and light. He sputtered and coughed as he continued to fight the water, but the current was stronger in the deep and it began to carry him away.

"Pauly!" screamed Rose. She started to run along the riverbank after him. "Pauly try and hang on to something!" she called out, even though she could not see anything for him to grab.

As she ran, Rose kept screaming for help, hoping that someone would hear her, but there was no one around. In desperation, she called out a prayer. "God save Pauly!" she shouted.

Pauly moved around a bend in the river and out of sight. Rose kept running. She ran around a clump of bushes that blocked the way. When she reached the riverbank once more, she saw that Pauly was now firmly in one place while the current moved quickly around him. "Pauly!" she called.

Pauly did not say anything. He just looked frightened. It was then that Rose could see he was hanging on to an old tree that was just under the surface. The tree seemed to be lodged on something deep under the water.

"Hang on Pauly," she called, as she looked around for something to help get him to shore. She could see that this was an area where a lot of garbage had collected from the higher water levels of the spring. There were plenty of bottles, cans and pieces of plastic everywhere. Rose searched among the litter for anything like a rope. She suddenly spotted a large old sheet lying on top of the dirt. It appeared muddied but not torn. She put Julia safely on a rock and picked up the sheet. Then tying one end of it to the lowest branch of a tree that grew right at the water's edge, she wrapped the other end securely around her arm. Next, Rose moved slowly towards Pauly.

Although the river was more narrow here, but it was also getting deeper fast. The water level was now up to Rose's waist, and she could feel the current threatening to sweep her away. She concentrated with every step and kept her footing. Finally, she was almost close enough to touch Pauly. "Grab the sheet," she said, holding out her arm as far as she could without getting in any deeper.

Pauly seemed frozen with fear and just blankly stared at her. "Pauly!" she shouted. "You have to save yourself! You have to reach out and grab this sheet!"

The boy looked into Rose's eyes, and knew she was right. Rose was always right. He reached over and grabbed hold of the end of the sheet with one of his hands. As he let go of the tree with his other hand, the current threatened to carry him off once more. Rose, who now had her right arm securely wrapped around the sheet, grabbed him and pulled him in. In a moment, they were both back on shore, exhausted and badly shaken.

Pauly sat in the soft green grass. He could feel the reassuring solid earth beneath him. At first, he could not say a word, but then eventually he looked at Rose and rambled, "I could have died! You saved me! Thanks Rose. You're my best friend!"

Rose could see that, at that moment, Pauly truly appreciated what she had done and felt deep gratitude. When he told her that she was his best friend, he was being sincere. Rose, however, did not bother to respond. She knew that despite what she had done, and what he said, Pauly had not changed. He would still never speak to her if someone else was around to see. Regardless of how he acted now, he would still not want to be seen with a *dirty Injun*.

# 18

The dark blue sedan pulled into a parking spot along the narrow Montreal street. "We have arrived," announced Marlon. Stuart looked down the long row of old European style stone buildings. Small hand painted signs hung above the many doors, marking shops, restaurants and art galleries.

The two men got out of the car. Marlon went to the trunk and began to remove the luggage. "We shall be staying here for several days," he said.

Stuart looked around in confusion. He did not see any signs for a hotel. "Staying where, exactly?" he asked his uncle.

"Right in front of you, Stuart," replied Marlon.

Stuart stared at the heavy old green door before him. He then looked up at the slightly faded hand-painted sign above it. It had gold lettering that simply read *L'abeille de Miel.*

"Could you take the bags please?" asked Marlon, who then closed the trunk of the car. He walked up to the door, while Stuart carried over the suitcases. Marlon knocked and they both waited.

It did not take long before the door opened and a well-kept older woman greeted them with a warm smile. "*Bonjour,*" she said.

"*Bonjour Madame,*" replied Marlon. "*Les renards sonts morts.*"

The woman's smile widened. "Oh, you are Marlon!" she exclaimed with a French accent. "Oh, I am so happy to meet you. My name is Claire." The silver bangles on her arms chimed as she put her arms around Marlon and kissed him on both cheeks.

"And this is my nephew Stuart," said Marlon.

"*Bonjour Madame*," said Stuart, who still held a suitcase in each hand. The woman leaned over to him and kissed him on both cheeks as well. "I am very happy to meet you, Stuart," she said. "Please *entrez*." The woman stood back inside the door to allow the two men inside.

Marlon and Stuart found themselves in a long hallway. They could see that the place was very clean and it had a slight aroma of pine. "Please come with me," said Claire, as she disappeared around a corner. They followed after her, and found themselves walking up a narrow staircase to the second floor. The stairs led to another hallway. Not far down the hall were two open doors side by side. Claire now stood in front of them. "These are your rooms," she said. "There is a washroom the next door down. If you should need anything, most of the time, I am downstairs in the *salon* or the kitchen. Also, my room is the one at the very end of the hall. You will find a key on one of the bureaus that opens the front door, so you may come and go as you please. I realize that you are doing some very important work, so I will not be in your way. But if you should need my help, just ask."

"Thank you Claire," said Marlon with a smile. "You are very kind."

Claire did not reply, but merely smiled back and then headed towards the stairs.

"Which one would you prefer?" asked Marlon, nodding towards the two open doors. "You may have first choice."

Stuart set down the luggage he was carrying. He stuck his head in one room, then the other. Both were modest, but tastefully decorated with French antiques. It all reminded him of the Paris vacations he had enjoyed with Jack, and he felt very comfortable about both rooms. "I suppose I shall take the one closest to the stairs," he said, choosing it at random.

"Good idea," said Marlon. "If the Duke's men catch up with us, they'll get to you first, and your screams will warn me. I may then have a chance to escape out the window."

Stuart laughed and asked, "And how do you know that I will not defeat them? What would happen if Robin Hood were faced by such peril? Of course, he would defeat them all, without as much as a drop of sweat from his brow."

Marlon smiled. "Yes that is exactly what Robin Hood would do. You made a perfect room choice, and I am a lucky man to have such a brave nephew," he said, patting Stuart on the shoulder. Marlon then yawned and added, "I am completely knackered and should take a short nap before we do anything further. Wake me when you are hungry, and we will ask Claire where to find the best restaurant." Marlon then picked up his suitcase and went into the room, closing the door behind him.

With Julia in hand, Rose climbed down to the place she called "The Princess Spot." She called it that because it seemed to her like a princess' balcony in a castle tower. There was a drawing in one of her books that showed such a balcony. It was the special place where the princess would stand and talk to the people below. Although she had learned in school that thousands of years ago a glacier carved out this small rock bowl in the side of the hill, it did not make the spot any less mysterious or magical. It was still as good as, or better than, any castle balcony.

The fragrant cedar trees that grew just above it had dropped many needles over the years, and created a soft orange floor. Rose liked to sometimes just sit and daydream in this little rock fortress where she always felt safe.

She stood and looked down the hill at the river below. "See Julia—see our subjects who have come to greet us." Rose was pretending that all of the rocks on the riverbank were people. "Hello people," she said, waving. She raised Julia's arm to wave also.

Suddenly, something flew down and landed in a nearby tree. It was a big black crow. "Hello crow," said Rose. "Have you come to hear my declaration?"

The crow said nothing, but just blankly looked at the little girl.

Rose knew that it was always important for a princess to make a declaration from the tower. She thought about what her declaration should be. There were many possibilities to choose from. Then she remembered something that had happened back in the springtime when she was at school. It was during afternoon recess, and she noticed that the children had all suddenly started running in a single direction. A girl, she didn't know, ran right past her crying, "Come on. It's a fight!"

Rose ran too. She ran up to the circle of children who were enthusiastically cheering. There was a small opening where she pushed in to see what all the excitement was about. Nothing prepared her for what she saw, and she knew that she would never forget it.

In the middle of the crowd were two older boys wildly thrashing and hitting at each other. Their faces were squished up and red, and there were tears in both of their eyes. Rose felt instantly sick. It wasn't about what they were doing. That was only a reflection of what was really going on. It was about what they were feeling—what they were all feeling. She looked at the children around who were cheering and chanting. She saw Lizzy on the other side laughing and clapping her hands. She saw the faces of the fighting boys locked in blind empty hatred. This was death! These children were dying all around her! They were all dying and they didn't care one bit!

Rose moved back from the circle. How could they not see it? How could they not feel it? What was wrong with these people? She then ran as far away as she could, to a place where she did not have to see the dying crowd any longer. This was a day she would always remember.

Looking up at the old crow, Rose asked. "What was wrong with them? Why did they not have sense to know what death smells like? Do they want to die, crow? Do they want to be gone forever?"

The crow said nothing, but just continued to stare out with its tiny eyes.

Rose then looked back down at the rocks below. She raised her right arm and said, "My people, I your princess, have a declaration to make. I now tell you that there will be no more fights—no more fights ever! If you fight, you will die. That is the law of God and Jesus, and there's no getting around it. The law is the law. Amen."

Rose turned again to the crow. "Go messenger," she said. "Go and spread the law throughout the land." She waved her arm and the crow flew away.

# 19

Marlon took a sip of red wine. "It's quite good," he said to Stuart. "Try it, and see what you think."

Stuart took a sip and rolled it briefly in his mouth before swallowing. "Yes it is excellent," he said. "Certainly equal to many I have sampled in France."

The two men sat in the outdoor café waiting for their food order. The evening was warm, and the sun was almost setting. Claire had recommended this restaurant for its authentic French Canadian cuisine.

"Tomorrow, we will be meeting with a contact here in Montreal. He is very important to this mission and should be able to provide us with pertinent information," said Marlon.

"Does that mean I will accompany you?" asked Stuart, hoping that he had not misinterpreted his uncle's use of the word 'we.'

"Yes," replied Marlon. "The protocol in Montreal is not so strict, and also I believe it would be best if we stuck together as much as possible."

Stuart was suddenly worried. Had his uncle guessed about what had happened in New York, and now didn't trust him on his own? The thought of Marlon feeling disappointed in him was troubling, and he felt he should say something. "Uncle, I am sorry I did not tell you earlier, but the Duke's man in New York spoke with me in the bar before you arrived. I suppose I was too embarrassed to say anything," he quickly blurted out.

Marlon looked directly at his nephew and softly smiled. "Do not doubt that you have my full trust Stuart. I have no worries or concerns about you speaking to that man or anyone else. I am certain that if you had said or done something that could have jeopardized our quest, then you would have realized it and told me about it immediately. You are an extraordinary young man, and I have every confidence in both your abilities and your judgments."

Stuart sighed at his uncle's words. No one, besides Jack, had ever put that much faith in him.

The waiter suddenly appeared with their plates of *tourtière* and set the food down before them. Stuart looked at the meat pie and laughingly said, "So far it looks much like home."

As the men began to eat, a woman carrying a lap dog sat down at a nearby table. When the waiter came over the dog snapped at him. The woman, who seemed to be a regular, placed her order, and then soothed the dog by feeding it eat a bread stick.

"It's spoiled," said Marlon, who then took another sip of wine. Stuart looked at him confused about what he was saying.

"The dog, I mean," explained Marlon. "It's spoiled and has become severely territorial, angry, paranoid and demanding. That is what the Bloodline can often be like."

Stuart laughed uncomfortably. It had been so deeply ingrained in him that the Bloodline was the noblest thing on earth, that it still made him a little uneasy to hear his uncle speak this way. He felt annoyed at himself for having these feelings.

"Think about this for a moment," said Marlon, pointing his fork in the direction of the lady and her pet, "think about that dog and its situation. It is an animal that lives in the world of man, but what does it truly know of this world?" He paused for a moment then added, "Nothing, or close enough to nothing. It knows nothing of the world in which it lives. Does it even begin to understand the full meaning or concept of the chair its owner sits upon? No. Can it understand the relationship between the woman and the waiter? No. Will it ever understand what a restaurant truly is and how it works? No. It comprehends almost nothing of the world in which it was born and in which it will die. It lives in a world without really living there at all; and in many ways one can say that the condition of man is somewhat the same."

"How is that?" asked Stuart, curious about where his uncle was taking this conversation.

Marlon took another bit of food, and said "We live in a world we think we know, but we know nothing at all. The Kingdom of God is the only reality—it is the one and only world, but like this dog, we cannot really see the world in which we live. The Kingdom is all around us, and it is also within us. When we give ourselves over to goodness, we see glimpses, or we catch its beautiful scent, and it is like a drink in the desert. However, we are still not there. We are still not really present in the Kingdom. Jesus was there. He tried to help people over. He tried to show them the way. He opened the door so they would no longer have to live like ignorant dogs, and could live like God. But they shut it. They shut that door for everyone when they rejected Him. Still, He did open it, and for a while some people looked in. That glimpse of the open door inspired so many. In some ways, we cannot fully comprehend how it truly made a difference in this world. I just pray that maybe now people are ready to have someone open the door again. Maybe this time it would remain wide open, and many of us could finally walk through to the other side."

Stuart was both astounded and moved by what his uncle had just said, "And do you believe that this little girl could open the door again? Is that what this is all about?"

Marlon looked at his nephew. There were tears in his eyes. "Yes," he replied. "If she is real, then she could open that door again. And now with the help of modern technology, she could reach so many people. We live in times when man has the capacity to destroy this planet. Both our souls and our world are in dire jeopardy. Perhaps—she would be able to save it all. I only pray that the prophecy is correct and that she is alive."

Stuart took another drink of his wine and looked at the sky. The bright blue had now softly faded and the red setting sun had painted the clouds a pale shade of pink. This girl was becoming more and more real. He could feel it. As the warm summer breeze caressed his face, Stuart couldn't help thinking that the more real the girl became, the more real he became with her.

* * *

"Rose!" Jeannie called. She had searched everywhere for her daughter and was now beginning to worry. It was very unlike Rose to be late for lunch, or any meal. Jeannie began to wonder if she should call the police.

It was then that she saw Rose appear over the hill. She was riding her bicycle fast down the side of the road. Suddenly without warning, it seemed that Rose had turned the bicycle towards the road and into the path of a pick-up truck. The truck swerved, narrowly missing her. The driver slowed, leaned out the window, swore at her and then sped off.

Rose returned to the side of the road, and continued peddling towards home. Jeannie ran out to meet her. "Rose!" she shouted. "You could have got yourself killed! What were you thinking?"

Rose leaned her bike against the wall and began to cry. "I didn't Mama! I didn't! Something else turned the bicycle handles. It wasn't me! Cross my heart! It wasn't me that did it Mama. I wouldn't do that!"

Jeannie could see how frightened and upset Rose was, and now felt bad that she had got so angry. "It's okay, but no more bike for a week. Now, come in and get your lunch. It's getting cold." Jeannie turned and went in the house.

Rose picked up Julia, who was sitting in the bicycle basket. "Mama doesn't believe me," she said to the doll. "She thinks that I just did something stupid. But you know it wasn't me. You know that I wouldn't do that. Something else turned those handlebars. Something wanted me to be dead—something evil. But don't worry Julia, 'cause evil can't win. That's the law."

* * *

A tiny bell above the door announced their entry as Marlon and Stuart entered the second-hand bookstore. They were immediately enveloped by the musty scent of old books. A dowdy middle-aged woman, who sat behind the counter, set down the book she had been reading and in a friendly voice exclaimed, "*Bonjour!*"

"*Bonjour Madame*," replied Marlon, who walked straight up to the counter. "I am here to see Father Vincent. Is he in?"

The woman's face changed. Her smile disappeared and she looked at Marlon with sympathy. "Oh you do not know," she said. "I am so sorry to tell you, but Father Vincent passed away only a week ago. There was a lovely, small and quiet funeral. I am sorry you did not know."

Marlon was visibly shaken. He had been told that this priest would provide him with crucial information necessary to locating the Golden Grail. He also knew that Father Vincent was the only one who possessed that knowledge, and now he was dead.

"How did he die?" Marlon asked, suddenly concerned that it could possibly have been murder. What was he to do if someone had killed the priest and taken the information? This would be disastrous.

"He died peacefully," the woman replied, "peacefully in his sleep. The Father did not suffer at all. To live eighty five years, and then to leave this world without pain or distress is certainly a blessing. He is now with the God he loved so much." The woman crossed herself. "Did you know him well? I have not seen you visit before, and the Father rented from me for a very long time."

"We knew each other from when we were both much younger men," Marlon lied. "Although we had not seen each other for many years, I considered him a very dear friend. We did correspond regularly, and we were working on a collaborative project. It was to be a book on the subject of Saint Lucia."

“Oh how tragic!” exclaimed the woman. “Father Vincent was a very knowledgeable man. How sad you were not able to begin your book, and on such a special saint too.”

“Well actually,” said Marlon, “I have compiled a great deal of material so far, and Father Vincent was working on his contribution. His plan was to hand over these papers to me so that I might be able to put them together with my own findings. It would certainly be a shame if I should have to continue on without the Father’s input. His thoughts would be of such value to this book. Would you by any chance know if the Father left behind any notebooks or papers? Without his assistance, I do not believe that I could possibly do proper justice to Saint Lucia.”

The woman looked at Marlon sadly. “I wish that I could help, but the Church came and took away all of his belongings shortly after he died. His few possessions all belong to them now. Perhaps if you contacted them, they would be able to help you. I am sure that they would want to see Father Vincent’s work published.”

This was bad news. Marlon knew that if he made inquiries at the church, it would simply arouse suspicion. They likely did not hold Father Vincent in high esteem, and may have even suspected his involvement in covert activities. Unsure what his next move should be, Marlon simply said to the woman, “Thank you. I am certain that the Church would be very interested in our work.” He then turned to Stuart and said, “This has been quite a shock. Perhaps, it would be best if we returned to the hotel.”

Stuart was feeling just as disappointed as Marlon. He did not want it to end like this. If the papers still existed, there must be a way to find them. Not knowing what else to do, Stuart desperately and silently prayed, *God, with all my heart I am seeking. Please help me to find.*

Marlon then sighed and said to the woman, “Well, I thank you for your help *Madame*. This has turned into a very sad day indeed.” He placed his hand on Stuart’s shoulder and said, “Come, my son.”

The two men turned and headed for the door. Just as they opened it, causing the little bell to ring once again, the woman shouted after them, "Wait *Monsieurs!*"

Marlon and Stuart stopped and turned towards the woman. She was holding up a small white booklet with red lettering on the front.

"Perhaps you would like to buy a copy of the Father's book of poetry to remember him by. He had printed twenty four copies only weeks before he passed. I am afraid that I still have all of them. Even at only fifty cents, they are not selling," said the woman, hopeful that she would make at least one sale today.

Marlon was suddenly full of hope again. A smile shot across his face. "Yes!" he exclaimed. "Yes, of course I will buy Father Vincent's poetry book! In fact, I will buy them all!"

* * *

Stuart sat in the chair in his uncle's room, carefully reading the small book of poetry. "I am unsure what exactly I should be searching for," he said.

Marlon sat on the bed and was looking through one of the other copies. "I cannot say yet," he answered. "But look for patterns, or something out of the ordinary."

As Stuart continued to read, he suddenly burst out laughing "This poetry is appalling," he said. "Listen to this:

> *For he will always be a pal to us,*
> *Our dear Saint Callimus de Lellis.*

Marlon laughed too. "Either Father Vincent was completely in denial about his poetic talents, or he did in fact leave us something in his poems. Let's keep looking."

"I am surprised that a Catholic Priest would be in the Underground," Stuart said as he turned the page.

Marlon looked over at his nephew. "Never forget Stuart, that there are good people everywhere—in every country, in every religion, in every group on earth. God scatters good people evenly around the world. Always remember to look past the person as a social construct, to what is in the heart. That is the only place you will find the truth. And that is the only part God recognizes—the only part that truly exists."

Stuart turned back to the index and studied it for a moment. Suddenly, he realized that there was something unusual. "Uncle," he said, "it appears that all of the poems are tributes to saints with the exception of one. On page 44, there is a poem that has an entirely different theme. It is a tribute to Notre Dame Cathedral here in Montreal."

Marlon quickly turned to the page and silently read through. Soon he began to smile. "I think that you may just have found it!" he exclaimed. He then read the poem aloud.

*To Notre Dame: Montreal*

*O' Notre Dame with single tower once above,*
*You sang praise to the lamb,*
*You sang praise to the dove.*

*Where are you now?*
*Far under the road,*
*Lost underground,*
*Lost in a code.*

*The only thing left,*
*To bring me to you,*
*A dark secret that runs*
*Through and through.*
*The old place*
*Where priests go to learn,*
*Of God and of Angels*
*So in hell they will ne'er burn.*

*Walk with me*
*Down the long dark hall,*
*Like 12 disciples walking,*
*But never to stall.*

*Except maybe to marvel*
*At your lovely grace,*
*A wall made of stone*
*With only one out of place.*

*O' Notre Dame,*
*So perfect were you!*
*Hiding your sweet secret*
*As all ladies do.*

Stuart was silently reading along from his own copy. He looked up at Marlon and asked, "Well, it is certainly a little *risqué* for a Catholic priest, but more importantly, what does it tell us, Uncle?"

Marlon stared at the words in front of him and thought for a moment. Finally, he said, "I do know some things about Notre Dame in Montreal. However, in this poem, the church is said to be underground and he talks only about a single tower. Notre Dame has twin towers and is quite prominently above ground. He must be talking about the original church that was torn down in 1830. It had been replaced with the great Notre Dame Basilica that stands today."

"Is there anything of the old church left underground?" asked Stuart.

"No," answered Marlon, "not of the church itself, but there is still the tunnel. There is an underground tunnel which once led from the church to the seminary. The original seminary still stands, and I believe it still provides access to that passageway."

"Could Father Vincent have hidden the information in the tunnel?"

Marlon closed the little book and replied, "All signs point to that conclusion—*a long dark hall* and an *old place where priests go to learn.*" Marlon became quiet as he contemplated the next plan of action. Suddenly, he threw down the book on the bed and said, "We need to get down to the tunnel Stuart, but first we must go shopping."

"What are we shopping for?"

"If I am right, we will certainly need a torch. Also a camera would be a good idea, and a Swiss army knife, in the case that we may require some sort of tool. I am unsure what difficulties we may encounter, so it is best to be as well prepared as possible." Marlon looked at his nephew. "I am very glad that you are coming with me, my son. It is reassuring to know that you will be there to help."

Stuart's heart beat faster. It was not merely the excitement of being part of a mysterious adventure that made him feel this way. It was also because this was a welcoming in the truest sense. Marlon was accepting him into the Underground, and Stuart felt a kind of pride he had never felt before. It was not the type of false pride he had learned from being of the Bloodline. This was different. It was the kind of pride that comes from deep within—a pride found at the very core of every human heart. This was the loving self-discovery of who he truly was, and who he would always be.

# 20

Robin Hood, with sword drawn, leapt out from behind the curtain and declared, "Maid Marion, I have come to rescue you."

Maid Marion dressed in a long flowing blue gown exclaimed, "Oh Robin Hood! Is it really you? Have you come to save me from the evil Sheriff of Nottingham?"

Suddenly, the Sheriff, all dressed in black, appeared from behind the curtain. "So Robin Hood, you think that you can beat me? Allow me to hurry you to your death." He drew his sword and the duel began.

Rose watched in wonderment as she sat in the fresh open air of the park. She had never seen anything like this! There were sometimes plays at school, but these were grown-ups with real costumes. They spoke their lines perfectly. It was almost as if it was all really happening.

For a moment, it seemed as if Robin Hood would die. Robin was down on the ground and the Sheriff was about to plunge his sword in. Rose did not want to look, but just as she was ready to close her eyes, Robin knocked the Sheriff's sword out of his hand, putting his own to the Sheriff's throat. The Sheriff then fell to his knees and begged for mercy.

Robin Hood decided to spare the Sheriff and turned to Maid Marion, but when he did, the Sheriff picked up his sword again and lunged at Robin's back. Robin Hood then quickly turned around and stabbed the Sheriff straight through the heart. The Sheriff of Nottingham fell to the stage floor.

"The Sheriff of Nottingham is dead!" Robin Hood proudly proclaimed. All of the children, including Rose, burst into applause and cheers.

"Oh Robin!" said Maid Marion. "You are my hero!"

The two embraced and the curtain closed on the trailer stage. Once again there was applause and cheering.

Robin Hood came out from behind the curtain and bowed to the crowd. He smiled at the children and announced, "We are the Old Oak Theatre Group for Youth. If you enjoyed our free production this afternoon, then perhaps you would like to be in a play yourself. We are giving acting classes all this month at the community center. At the very end of the course, we will be putting on a play that your parents and others will be able to see. Would any of you like to learn to be an actor and star in a play?"

All of the children waved their hands and yelled that they wanted to be in a play. Rose had her hand up too. More than anything she wanted to be in a play. She wanted to be a part of this magic.

Robin Hood gestured with his hands for the children to quiet down. "Well, if you would like to join us, we have some application forms here." He pointed over to Maid Marion who was holding up a stack of papers. "You just have to take the form to your parents, have Mom or Dad fill it out, and return it along with a ten dollar fee to the community hall this week anytime between 9:00 in the morning and 2:00 in the afternoon. All of the information is right there on the form, and if your parents have any questions, there is a number they can call."

Rose was instantly crushed. To be in the play, you had to pay ten dollars. She knew that her mother did not have the money. Rose would not be in the play, just like she would not take dance lessons from the lady on Hill Street, or piano lessons, or any other kind of lessons that she wished for. Tears began to well up in her eyes, but she stopped them before they could fall. There were too many people around. If she cried, someone would see and make fun of her. As all of the children began to crowd the stage to get a form, Rose discreetly got up and walked away in the other direction.

* * *

Wishing to appear just part of the crowd, Marlon raised the camera to his eye and snapped a photo along with the other tourists. He and Stuart stood across the street to get a proper view of the magnificent cathedral in front of them. The noble twin towers that rose up towards the heavens seemed indestructible. High above the three arches that marked the three doors were three figures carved in stone—in the very center stood Mary. Her head was surrounded by twelve shining golden stars, and she watched over the people below, welcoming them with her arms wide open.

"She is beautiful," said Stuart.

"Yes indeed," agreed Marlon. "Our beautiful mother!"

They stood in silence and simply stared at the amazing sight. The sunshine alighted each of each Mary's stars, and she somehow looked so warm and alive, in spite of being carved from stone.

Marlon could not help but think about the real woman, who lived so long ago. It was unimaginable what she must have gone through. How could her heart not have shattered into a million pieces as she sat at the foot of that cross? He sighed to think that such love could have survived such pain. The world owed her more than a simple monument. It owed her everything.

Although reluctant to break the spell that held them there, Marlon knew that time was of the essence. "We must keep to our task, Stuart. The seminary is right beside the church. It is the oldest building in Montreal, and provides access to the tunnel," he said, stuffing the camera into the canvas bag that he carried on his shoulder.

Stuart followed Marlon across the street and then along an old stone wall to an iron gate. Just above the gate was a colorfully painted crest with a geometric figure in the middle and two lions on either side. The two men both recognized the symbols, and simply looked at each other knowingly.

Marlon pushed gently on the gate and it easily opened. Checking to ensure no one was around they then slipped inside of the enclosed grounds. The pathway in front of them led directly to a classic carved entrance that stood in stark contrast to the rustic fieldstone walls.

Stuart was surprised when his uncle did not hesitate to walk right up the stone steps and boldly open one side of the large double doors. They both went straight in and closed the door behind them.

A strange sterile smell was immediately noticeable and made them both feel uncomfortable. They carefully looked around and to their relief saw no sign of anyone. Marlon knew that it was only a matter of time before someone would come by. "Quickly," he said to Stuart, "we must find the stairs to the cellar."

Stuart checked behind the door closest to him, but found only a closet. Before he could look behind a second door, his uncle, who had gone further down the corridor, signaled to him that he had found the entrance. Stuart hurried over.

Marlon took out two flashlights from the canvas bag. "Take this torch," he said, handing one to Stuart. They both switched on their flashlights and headed down the stone steps into the dark abyss. After descending down three separate sets of stairs, they finally reached the lowest level. Stuart thought about how far underground they now were and couldn't help but be reminded of Dante's descent into Hell. As he shone his light over the walls, he could see that the arched tunnel had been constructed with perfect precision. Each stone seemed to fit tightly against the next. No amateur had built this underpass. It was a work of art despite being cold, damp and smelling of things long past. As they moved slowly along the dark corridor, Stuart asked, "What are we looking for?"

"If you remember Stuart, the poem contained a single number. It was the number 12. We should perhaps look for anything that repeats twelve times." Marlon moved his light around the walls and floor as he searched for something that could possibly be relevant. The tunnel was so bare and empty that it was difficult to decide what it could be. The silent stone walls were not revealing any secret.

Stuart continued to shine his own light around the tunnel, and could see nothing of interest. He then turned the beam towards the ceiling and was excited by what he saw. "I think I've got it!" he exclaimed. "Look up, Uncle!"

Marlon shone his light on the curved ceiling. There were pipes and wires that ran through to carry electricity and plumbing to the seminary above. He then looked to where Stuart had fixed his light. There, on one of the pipes, was a small inconspicuous red number '2'. A mark that could have easily just been left by a plumber.

"If we follow this pipe, then we may find subsequent numbers," said Stuart.

"You have found our only clue yet," responded Marlon, "and I believe you are right. We should investigate further."

They walked along and sure enough, more red numbers appeared in order. When they reached the pipe with the number 12, they found themselves at a dead end. The doorway was sealed by a cement wall. "Do you think we need to break through the wall?" asked Stuart, thinking only how on earth they could possibly accomplish this.

"I don't believe so," said Marlon. "I can't imagine such an old priest building a cement wall. If you remember, the poem spoke of a stone out of place. Look around and see if you can find one."

Stuart and Marlon began to run their hands over the walls, testing for a loose or out of place stone. "Here!" suddenly exclaimed Stuart. Marlon looked to the place where the light was shining. At the bottom of the wall was a single inconspicuous stone that jutted out only slightly from the rest. He took the Swiss army knife from the bag and began to pry it loose at the edges.

Stuart set down his flashlight, and grabbed hold of the stone with both hands. He then easily dragged it all the way out. Marlon shone the light on the opening. He put his hand inside and pulled out what appeared to be a brown envelope wrapped in clear plastic. Looking at it only briefly, he then quickly stuffed it into his bag. "We need to get out of here as quickly as possible," he said to Stuart.

Stuart put the stone back, and they headed for the stairs. Once they reached the top, Marlon took both flashlights and placed them back in the bag. He then slowly opened the door and looked out. There still seemed to be no one around. He motioned to Stuart, and they began to make a move towards the exit.

Just as they had reached the front foyer, a voice suddenly shouted from behind them. "*Arrêtez! Arrêtez!* "

Marlon and Stuart turned and saw an austere looking young priest staring right at them. He was dressed in traditional robes, and had large round glasses that magnified his eyes, making him look like an angry owl.

Marlon immediately put on a large friendly smile and exclaimed, "Oh hello there! What a magnificent cathedral you have here. May I take your picture?" He pulled the camera from his bag.

"This is not part of the Basilica," said the young priest sternly. He had only the slightest French accent.

"Oh dear me, it is not?"

"No it is not!" The priest eyed Marlon suspiciously. "This is the seminary."

"Oh Morton, do you hear that. It is the seminary. Jolly good!" Marlon looked directly at Stuart.

Stuart took his uncle's hint and began to play along. "Oh, the seminary! That is exceptional!" replied Stuart.

Marlon saw the young priest pause and look for a long moment at Stuart. Marlon, still smiling like a happy tourist then took a step forward and said to the priest, "You see, Father, it surely must be providence that we have wandered into the seminary. My son, Morton, and I are vacationing from England. We were simply sightseeing before finding ourselves here. But the strangest part is that Morton has been telling me for some time now that he has felt, deep within his heart, a calling to the priesthood. I finally agreed that we would look into it when we returned to England. The fact that we are accidentally here now must certainly be a sign."

"Yes a sign," added Stuart.

The young priest looked at Stuart again and his face broke out into a smile revealing the full extent of his significant over-bite. "You feel that you have been called?" he asked Stuart.

"Oh yes," he said, smiling sweetly. "Ever since I was a boy, I have dreamed of being a priest. Although I have been conveying my feelings for some time, my father is only now beginning to understand my passion."

"That is very true," said Marlon. "But now, after being here and meeting you, I am almost certain that this is my son's calling. After wandering into a seminary of all places, I think Morton must be right. However, I would still prefer that he speak to a priest first about exactly what such a choice would entail. Do you think you could help by counseling Morton perhaps sometime tomorrow? Today, our agenda is completely full, but tomorrow would be perfect. We are near the end of our stay here, I am afraid, and are shortly due back in England. I realize that this is a great favor to ask and that you may not have the time…"

"Yes of course—of course I have the time," said the priest eagerly.

"Oh jolly good!" exclaimed Marlon. "What do you think Morton? Is this a good idea?"

Stuart looked at the priest and saw him blush. "It is a perfect idea father," he said. "Why do I not come back tomorrow afternoon?"

The priest grinned from ear to ear. "Two o'clock would be a good time."

"Then two it shall be," smiled Stuart.

Marlon and Stuart, eager to get out of there as quickly as possible, turned and began to walk away. Stuart was reaching for the door latch, when the priest suddenly shouted, "No, do not leave!"

Marlon and Stuart stopped and looked back at the priest who was no longer smiling. Instead, he now had a look of serious concern on his face. They were both hoping his suspicions had not somehow been revived.

"Morton, what is your full name, so I might put it in my diary?" the priest simply asked.

Marlon quickly answered for Stuart. "The name's Higginsbottom," he called out, "Morton Higginsbottom."

Once they were outside the gate and headed down the sidewalk, there was a great sense of relief between them. "So Uncle, do I really look like a Morton Higginsbottom to you?" Stuart jokingly asked.

Marlon laughed, "My son, if you looked anything like a Morton Higginsbottom, we would never have been able to get by that sentry. Now let's return to the hotel and see what is in that envelope."

# 21

Rose was lying on her stomach in Mrs. Warren's backyard. The summer sun was warm on her back as she closely examined the ground in front of her. She marveled at the strange almost hidden world that was there. The plants and grasses grew in such a way that there were little roads and pathways everywhere. An occasional ant would wander by then disappear under some leaves or in a patch of grass.

Rose turned to Julia and said, "What if we were ants? Do you know that everything small would look so big, and everything big would disappear? An ant can see a speck of dirt, but it's too small to see the big things. It can't see a house or a car. If we were ants, we wouldn't be able to see anything that wasn't little. We wouldn't see all the things that we can see now."

A little honeybee flew by her head and Rose called after it:

*Bless you, bless you bonnie bee*
*Say, when will my wedding be?*
*If it be tomorrow day,*
*Take your wings and fly away.*
*Fly away east or fly away west,*
*And show me where he lives, who loves me the best!*

Rose waited to see if the bee would return, but it was gone.

As she continued to lounge in the grass, the intense summer sun began to get a little too hot for her skin, and she found herself suddenly craving a cool drink of water. Rose quickly jumped up and ran to the kitchen door hoping that her mother would be there.

Jeannie cleaned Mrs. Warren's house on Tuesdays, and had to bring Rose along during the summer months when there was no school. Rose was never allowed inside, but had to wait in the yard or on the porch if it was raining. Mrs. Warren was an older lady who had been married a long time, but had no children. She did not trust Rose in her house where she had a large collection of shiny breakable objects.

Rose stood at the screen door and peered in. "Mama," she whispered. "Mama, I need a drink of water."

Jeannie, who was washing dishes in the sink, looked over at Mrs. Warren, who sat at her kitchen table reading a magazine. Mrs. Warren looked at Jeannie and said, "Of course get her a drink, and have her come in. She may drink it here at the table with me."

Jeannie was surprised. This was very unlike Mrs. Warren.

Rose, who heard everything, cautiously opened the door and stepped inside.

"Come, my dear," said Mrs. Warren. "Come and sit here with me."

Rose slowly went over and sat at the table. Jeannie set a fresh glass of water in front of her. Rose put Julia down in the table and took the glass in both hands. She drank with the hastiness of a thirsty child.

"And what is your dolly's name?" asked Mrs. Warren with a smile.

"Julia," answered Rose.

"Well, isn't Julia very interesting," said Mrs. Warren.

Rose did not know what to say to that. Julia was not interesting, she was beautiful. Still, she knew that Mrs. Warren would probably not like it if she were to disagree with her. It was best not to say anything.

"And what do you want to be when you grow up?" asked Mrs. Warren with an even bigger smile.

Rose thought about it. There was only one thing she could think of that she really wanted to be. "A superhero," she answered.

Mrs. Warren started laughing with delight, and Rose started laughing too. "That is perfectly charming," Mrs. Warren said. "A superhero—how very cute!"

Rose finished the water that was left in her glass. She was happy that she had made Mrs. Warren laugh. She had never seen her laugh before. Without thinking about it, Rose suddenly asked, "What will you name the baby?"

Mrs. Warren did not laugh again. Instead, she just sat with her mouth open in shock. It did not take long for the shock to wear off, and then Mrs. Warren looked angry and afraid. "No one knows yet! Not even my husband! I have told no one! How did you know?"

Rose realized that she had said the wrong thing. Without answering, she grabbed Julia and ran outside.

In the kitchen, a shaken Mrs. Warren said to Jeannie, "Do not let that child inside of my house again!"

* * *

Marlon tore the plastic from the brown envelope. He then opened it, removed the papers from inside and began to read. Stuart watched as a glowing smile appeared across his uncle's face.

"This is it!" exclaimed Marlon. "This is the genealogy!" He handed it to Stuart so that he might see.

Stuart looked it over quickly. They had done it! Together they had found the map to the greatest treasure in the history of man!

Marlon sat down on the bed. He was feeling overcome with emotion. "There are place names!" he said. "There are even place names!" He turned his eyes towards the ceiling and exclaimed, "Thank you Father Vincent!"

Stuart still held the papers in his hands. He did not want to set them down. "We will be leaving tomorrow then?" he asked, anxious to finally see the end of their quest within reach.

"Yes," replied Marlon, still reeling with emotion. "Tomorrow we will set out for Ontario."

Stuart suddenly thought about the Duke and felt a little worried. How would they keep her hidden from him? "Are you concerned about the Duke? What if he finds out?" he asked.

Marlon was still smiling. "No," he replied. "The Duke does not frighten me. After all, he is not what he appears to be."

"But he has so much wealth and influence," said Stuart, who was beginning to feel a little doubt about the outcome of their mission. "He has always gotten what he wanted. Why would this be any different?"

"Does he really have power?" Marlon laughed. "Do you not remember what I told you about the Kingdom of God? That is the real world, my son. The Duke's world is make-believe. Is he a man of influence and power in the Kingdom? No Stuart. In the Kingdom, he is weak and dying."

Stuart thought for a moment about what his uncle had just said. It was beginning to make sense to him. After all, society was nothing but a fabricated trick of the imagination. It was all smoke and mirrors. What if there really was a Kingdom of God—a world that was not a fabrication, but eternal and perfect. Just who would any of them really be in this world of Truth?

"Think of it this way," said Marlon, "we come into God's world with only one lasting thing. We have only our soul and that is all. Throughout our lives there is only one thing we can keep and no one can take away. That is again our soul. *When we have shuffled off this mortal coil,* we can still only take one thing with us, and that is our soul. If you give away that, what do you have left? If you give away your soul, then not only do you now have nothing, but you are nothing. You are dead in the truest sense of the word.

"That is why the Duke is nothing more than a sad, weak and dying man. I don't believe that he has enough soul left to call his own any longer. He is just slowly disappearing. His wealth and power are merely illusions that drag him further towards the final abysm. Once he is gone from this earthly world, he is gone forever. That is true death, Stuart, and that is what Jesus warned us about."

Stuart looked down at his father's ring. It was suddenly no longer as shiny and impressive as it had once been before. It now just looked rather silly and garish, much like a piece of children's play jewelry. Stuart pulled the ring from his finger, and put it in his jacket pocket. It was only then that he realized how heavy the stone really was. He wiggled his bare fingers. They felt good. There was a mark where the ring was, but he knew that it would soon disappear. He then looked up at his uncle who was smiling at him.

"Does that feel better, my son?" asked Marlon.

"Yes," smiled Stuart. "It feels just like freedom should."

* * *

The next morning, Stuart was up early and had packed his things. The night before Marlon had entrusted him with the brown envelope, which both frightened and delighted him. He slept with it under his pillow all night long and only now set it down when he had no other choice.

Stuart was feeling as impatient as a child. He wanted to move on and finally reach that place where they might find the Golden Grail. Convincing himself that was not too early to wake his uncle, he went out into the hall where he knocked on Marlon's door. He waited, but there was no answer.

Slowly opening the door, he peered inside. Marlon was nowhere to be seen. Stuart entered the room and looked around. The bed was neatly made, and there were toiletries on the old oak bureau. He opened the mirror doors of the wardrobe and saw that all of Marlon's clothes were still there. It seemed that his uncle had disappeared.

Stuart began to panic. What if the Duke's men had followed them? Could they have taken his uncle while he slept? If that were the case, then surely they would have taken Stuart also. After all, he was the one who had the information. He quickly searched around the room for clues, but found nothing out of the ordinary.

Stuart went out into the hall and tried to collect his thoughts. Who would he call? Where should he search? He turned to go down the stairs, when suddenly he heard a woman's voice coming from behind him. "*Mon Cheri*, please stay longer," she said.

As he was turning around, he heard his uncle reply, "Believe me when I say that I wish I could beautiful lady, but duty calls."

At the end of the hall just outside of Claire's room, Stuart saw Claire dressed in a red satin robe with her arms around his uncle's neck. For a moment, they didn't seem to notice him at all, but then they turned their heads towards him. Claire smiled and waved. "Good morning Stuart!" she called out happily.

Marlon kissed Claire goodbye, and she went back into her room closing the door. He then headed down the hall towards Stuart. "So sorry I'm late. I still need to pack up my things. Won't be but a moment," chimed Marlon.

Stuart did not know whether he was more relieved or amused. "Well Uncle," he said trying to sound slightly irate, "I believe that you have some explaining to do."

Marlon laughed and winked. "This body may be old, but it's not dead yet, my son."

# 22

The water exploded the sun's reflection into a myriad of dancing shimmers, and it looked to Rose as if someone had filled the river with beautiful diamonds. She watched as a kingfisher suddenly dove past the sparkling surface and disappeared. He soon reappeared with something shiny in his beak. It seemed as though he were fishing for the diamonds. She called after him, "Remember what happened to the crow, Mr. Kingfisher. Don't let a fox flatter you and take your diamond!"

As Rose began to walk along the riverbank with Julia tightly in her hand, there was a feeling of calm and peace in the air. When she reached the hill that led up to the bridge, she carefully climbed the steep embankment. Once on the bridge, Rose looked down at the water below. It was looking different in this place. The shade from the big trees kept the sun from reflecting here, and the water was now dark and murky.

Rose was so absorbed in thinking about the river that she did not notice Glen and his friends until they were already on the bridge. At first, she thought she would have to run again, but when she saw their faces, she somehow knew that this time, they would not chase her. She was right. Instead, they simply passed by, but as they did Glen yelled, "Nice shoes Injun! Shoppin' at the dump agin?" The boys all laughed together.

Rose looked down at her simple canvas running shoes. They were definitely cheaper than what most of the other children wore, and now one of them had developed a hole in the toe. Her right toe was almost peeking completely out. Rose hid that one behind her leg and looked down at the river again. She felt like crying.

Before her eyes could fill with tears, Rose was suddenly struck by the feeling that someone was watching her. She raised her head and looked to her left. At the edge of the bridge only a few yards away, there stood two men silently staring at her. Time seemed to stand still as she sensed their very thoughts. She knew immediately why they had come. Those men had traveled a long way to find her. They came to see only her, and were now happy and relieved that she was there. They could feel her presence, and they recognized her.

The dark sadness of defeat, that crushed her spirit only a moment ago, was gone. It had been pushed out by the glorious calm and strength that now filled her with life. These two men could see her, and knew who she was! That mattered! In a world where even your own mother did not know who you were—that mattered so much. They were not strangers like everyone else in her life. They recognized her and loved her for it! "Friends," she whispered into Julia's ear.

As she stood on the bridge, Rose suddenly became aware of the heat of the sun upon the crown of her head. It reminded her that it was almost time for lunch, and she shouldn't make her mother worry by being late. It was time to go home. In her mind, she simply thought the words, *it is done*. She then silently turned from the two men and headed east along the old road.

* * *

Stuart followed his uncle, who seemed to know the way to go. He expected that they would stop at one of the homes along the street, but they passed each one by. Instead, Marlon turned down an old tree lined road which seemed barely used anymore.

"Where are we going Uncle?" asked Stuart.

"I am unsure," replied Marlon. "I am simply going where God is telling me to go."

Stuart wanted to have complete faith in his uncle, but he couldn't help doubting the possibility that Marlon would be

154

getting directions from God. However, he said nothing. Even if there was doubt in his mind, Stuart knew it was best if he kept it to himself. He had doubted so much before, and had been wrong every time. Why should this time be any different?

They silently walked along the old road which seemed very long and winding. Stuart was just about to wonder aloud if they were getting any closer, when Marlon suddenly stopped. The two men were now standing at the edge of a bridge. In the middle, they saw a little girl leaning against the metal railing and staring down into the water. On the opposite side, a group of boys were walking by, and when she looked up at them, they hurled an insult. The little girl said nothing, but just looked back down into the river.

Stuart could see that her feelings had been hurt and wondered if he should do something. He was just about to ask his uncle about what he should do, when suddenly the girl turned and looked directly at them. It was astounding! She wasn't looking at them as if they were strangers. She seemed to know who they were, and why they were there. Stuart could not believe what he was now feeling. Overcome by a sense of calm connectedness, it was as if he were being lovingly melted into a warm shimmering pool of living light. All time and space disappeared, and he found himself resting in a place of ineffable contentment. As he continued to stare, the girl then slowly turned and without a word, walked in the opposite direction.

Stuart was immobile at first, but then he wanted only to follow her. "Uncle, should we not go after her?" he asked, when Marlon did not seem to be moving.

"No," said Marlon. Stuart was surprised by the answer. He looked over at his uncle and saw that his face was wet with tears.

Stuart was beginning to get a little frantic now that the girl was almost out of sight. He wanted her back. "But, do we know where she lives? We need to find where she lives!"

"That is not necessary," replied Marlon. "It is time to go home now."

Stuart was confused. "Home? But why? We need to go after her uncle! Did you not see her…her clothes…her shoes?

Did you not see how those boys treated her? We cannot leave her here!" He was now becoming upset. The idea that they should just walk away made no sense at all. Also the little girl's situation couldn't help but remind Stuart of his own school days. All he wanted was to protect her from the same pain.

"We cannot take her anywhere," said Marlon. "That is not why we came."

"Why then?" asked Stuart, feeling frustrated. The little girl was already out of sight. "Why did we come all this way and work so hard to find her? How can we just walk away and leave her like this?"

"We came for that single reason, my son—only to find her—to see her—to know that she saw us. Besides making certain that the genealogy gets into the right hands, this is all that we can do. She is truly of The Vine and she must be left here."

Stuart would not let this drop. He still could not understand what his uncle was talking about. "Why must we leave her? She cannot live like this. We have to take her back. We can find a safe place where we could all live together—the girl, you, me and Jack. We could be her family, and keep her safe from the Duke." Stuart thought about the Duke, and how upset he would be to see that she was not his Aryan ideal. He then thought about the white doves that the Duke used as sacrifices in his occult ceremonies, and was afraid for her life. They had to keep her safe.

"She will be safest from the Duke if she is left here. She belongs only to God and this is the place chosen for her." Marlon could see that Stuart was still having a difficult time understanding. He put his hand on his shoulder and said, "In the Book of John, there is an answer. The question is missing, but the answer was written down. The question that was asked of Jesus was why his life had been so full of suffering? Why was he not born into a family of wealth, and given great opportunities instead of the poverty and pain he knew. His answer was that He was the True Vine and that God was the Gardener. Of God He says,

*He cuts off every branch in me that bears no fruit, while every branch that does bear fruit he prunes so that it will be even more fruitful.*


"Can you see Stuart? Part of me also wishes we could take her from here, but she is The Vine. What she suffers is for God's Great Work. God cuts away anything that will not bear fruit, so that when it does come time for her, her branches will be full to perfection. She is being prepared so that when the time is right, she will be the tree that feeds an entire world. We cannot interfere with the work of God. That little girl belongs to God, and to God alone."

Stuart thought about what Marlon was telling him. He then remembered the wonderful things he had felt when the girl simply looked at him. What if the whole world could feel that? It would change everything! It had certainly changed him forever. "I understand," he said, surrendering to his uncle's reasoning.

They stood for a while longer, and Stuart stared down the road in the direction where the girl had gone. For a moment, he only wished that she would come back, but at the same time, he knew that this could not happen. Marlon was right and she had to go on her own way. "Let us go home, Uncle," he said a little sadly.

Marlon put his arm around his nephew. "Do not feel sorrow, my son," he said. "We have been given a great gift today—a gift straight from God." The two men then headed back the way they had come.

# 23

It was a lovely sunny day as Stuart walked along the bustling streets of Greenwich Village. The people who passed him all seemed to be smiling, and there was a strong sense of community in the air. It didn't feel anything like a big city. It felt like a good place to be.

Marlon was meeting with his New York contact one last time. Before he left, he told Stuart that while he was gone, he should take some time for himself, and enjoy a few of the sights. They were to meet up in two hours, and towards evening they would be boarding their flight to England.

Stuart stopped to look in a shop window. As he stood staring at the various beads and bobbles that glittered in the window, he began to wish that Jack was there also. Jack would have loved Greenwich Village. Stuart smiled when he thought about how supportive Jack had been about everything. He never questioned Stuart's need to spend time with his uncle, or even to get involved in this dangerous work. When Stuart told him about leaving for America, he never complained. Jack was willing to make sacrifices without a second thought. Stuart knew that he must, at the very least, bring back a nice gift to show his appreciation.

He began to check through the shops, but after looking through several, could not find anything that he felt was just right. Eventually, Stuart began to feel a little tired. He knew that it was getting closer to the time when he would have to meet up with Marlon again. He was just about to turn around and go back to a small shop where he had seen a suitable but not so interesting shirt, when he noticed a small make-shift art gallery set up in one of the alleyways.  He quickly walked over and began to examine the unusual paintings that where hanging on old boards and leaning against the brick wall. They were all very modern, mostly abstract and extremely colorful.

Stuart squatted down to have a closer look at a green spiraling one that rested against the wall. Suddenly, he had the feeling that someone was watching him. When he turned his head, he saw a pair of sandaled feet at the bottom of a linen robe. Slowly, he looked up, and there, standing over him, was a man with a thick brown beard and wild long hair. He was smiling warmly and holding up two fingers in the peace sign. Stuart's first thought was *Jesus?*

"Wwwhoa, peace man!" exclaimed the man, happily.

Stuart silently laughed at himself as he realized that this was not Jesus, but rather just the artist behind the paintings. He stood up and replied, "Hello."

"You looking for anything special?" the artist asked.

"Why yes," replied Stuart. "I need a gift for someone."

"Outta sight man! You're English! Cool!" the artist exclaimed with delight.

Stuart laughed. It was amusing to imagine that anyone would think that being British was cool. "Yes, I am," he said. "I've been vacationing, and I require a gift to take back with me. This gift is for someone very important."

"Groovy!" said the man, who then began to look around at his various works. "Ummm…how's about something psychedelic? Does this important person dig it in a far out kinda way?" The artist held up a painting that was full of brilliant swirling colors.

"Oh, that is very nice," said Stuart politely. "But would you by any chance happen to have something with a unicorn? I know it is probably not your thing, but I should, at the very least, ask."

"Oh man!" replied the artist, grabbing his head dramatically. "Man, do I have a unicorn!"

Stuart was surprised by the artist's answer, and also excited to know that he did indeed have such a painting.

"But I gotta warn you," said the artist in a very serious tone. "It was a real crazy trip. You know what I mean? I don't know what was in that shit, but man, it blew my mind. Blew it straight to kingdom come and back! So I drop this shit—and the next thing I know, I'm painting—just furious, crazy painting! Whoa man, was I painting! Don't get me wrong. It was a real good trip…just…you know…crrrrazy."

For a moment, the artist went silent and Stuart wondered if he was off on another "trip." Then without a word, he suddenly walked to the back of his patchwork store. He rifled around and returned with medium sized canvas in hand. The painting was turned away so that Stuart could not see it. The artist looked him in the eye and said, "I gotta warn you, man. This one was freaking people out. I had to put it back there, where nobody could see 'cause it was scaring my customers away. And like, you know, I don't worship mammon or anything, but we all gotta eat. Are you ready to take a look?"

Stuart wanted very much to see the painting. "Not to worry," he told the artist. "I do not frighten easily."

"Okay man, here it is," said the artist, turning the painting around.

Stuart was stunned by what he saw. There was certainly a unicorn. It was a large white magnificent looking creature, but the background was not lush and green as the unicorn's habitat is usually depicted. Instead it was a rocky desert. Still, that was not the strangest part. The painting also had a huge shiny black gorilla. It was a massive and muscular looking thing. There must have been a battle between the two because the unicorn had red bloody scratches down its shoulder and a small bloody wound on its flank. There was, however, no doubt about the victor. The unicorn's head was lowered and its great white horn was driven straight through the gorilla's thick neck. The ape's small black eyes were open, but only in blank empty death. He had most definitely been defeated, and had met with his complete and final end.

"I know man," said the artist apologetically. "Like I said, it was a crazy trip." He turned and was ready to put the painting back.

"Wait!" exclaimed Stuart. "It is absolutely perfect!"

The artist looked very surprised, and then a large smile crossed his face. "Groovy!" he said, "I'll wrap it up."

* * *

Standing with his uncle in London Heathrow Airport, Stuart hesitated to say goodbye. He knew that, now back in England, they would both be headed into more dangerous territory, but he was worried mostly for Marlon. Stuart did not feel right leaving him on his own.

"Uncle, are you certain that you want me to take the papers to Scotland? Perhaps we should go together," said Stuart, hoping he could change his uncle's mind.

"You know that would be a mistake," said Marlon. "The Duke would most certainly have us followed just as I am certain he is now having us watched. No, you must go, and I will create a diversion of sorts. If he suspects that I have information, he will not be watching you. He will be expecting that I went to America for good reason, and will be keeping a close eye on me. When he questions you, you need only act the part of the bumbling spy, who found nothing."

Stuart adjusted the wrapped painting he held under his arm. He still had a very bad feeling about letting his uncle go alone, but he knew that Marlon would not be swayed. Stuart suspected that it was not just about getting the papers to Scotland. Marlon's plan was also designed as a way to keep him safe. Although he wanted to protest, he knew that there would be no point.

"Go home and see Jack," said Marlon. "The Duke will certainly contact you there. When he does, tell him that you found nothing on our trip, but that you have not given up and will be meeting with me again soon. When you leave for Scotland, he must only assume that you are coming to see me, so you will not be followed. I will call you tomorrow morning to signal you to leave. Also, I know your phone will be bugged, so I will not speak openly, but you will know what I mean."

Stuart silently nodded.

"And one more thing," said Marlon, "when you leave, take Jack with you and do not return. Here is the phone number of a lawyer who has the details of a bank account that is in both of your names. You may go anywhere you wish, but I suggest you leave the U.K. completely. It would be too dangerous for you to remain." Stuart accepted the slip of paper and stuffed it in his pocket.

It suddenly became clear to Stuart that he might never see his uncle again, but he didn't want to believe it. He put his free arm around Marlon and hugged him. Marlon hugged him back. When he released his nephew he said, "Now go. You still have some work to do Sir Robin."

Stuart watched as his uncle walked away. He could not bring himself to turn and go while Marlon was still in sight. Just before disappearing out a door, Marlon looked back and waved. Stuart raised his hand in a salute. He still only wished that he could follow after and protect his uncle.

Stuart sighed and turned to go to the parking lot. As he did, he noticed a woman with long black hair and dark glasses walking directly towards him. His first thought was that the Duke had somehow learned that he possessed the documents, and that this could be some kind of trap.

Stuart was startled when the woman suddenly threw her arms around his neck and kissed him on his mouth. "Don't you recognize me, Stu?" she asked laughingly, as she let go of him and removed her sunglasses.

"Alexa!" said Stuart, who was so happy to see her. "I had no idea it was you. You look completely different."

"Good," responded Alexa. "I don't want anyone to recognize me. I'm on my way to Spain where Amando is waiting for me. We are going to be married there."

Stuart smiled at her. "Congratulations! I am so happy for both of you," he said.

"Do you know that it is because of you that I am leaving?" Alexa reached up and ran her hand affectionately down the side of his face.

Stuart smiled at the touch of her small soft hand. He was surprised by what she had said and asked, "How is that?"

Alexa tilted her head and looked warmly into his eyes. "You inspired me, Stuart. I knew how much courage it took for you to defy the Duke. You chose faith over your own security. Seeing you break free from all of that Bloodline madness gave me the courage to break free also. I now have the strength to follow my heart. I can't live in the Duke's world anymore. Amando is my world and that is where I must go."

Stuart was amazed. He had thought of Alexa as nothing but courage. She had seemed so strong at a time when he had felt so weak. The idea that he had somehow managed to inspire her filled him with pride. He looked at her beaming face and said, "Give me your hand."

Alexa smiled and held out her left hand. Stuart then removed his father's ring from his pocket, and placed it on her finger. It was far too large and threatened to fall off. He then closed her hand tightly into a fist to keep it in place. For a few moments, he just held her hand in his own. "It is a wedding gift," he said smiling. "When you reach Spain, you may sell it, and put the money towards a new home for yourself and your husband."

Alexa looked at him with tears in her eyes. She gently kissed him on the cheek and said, "Thank you my dearest friend. You came into my life just when I needed you most, and now, I will miss you terribly. One day, you must come and visit us in Spain, and be sure to bring Jack with you."

Stuart adjusted the package under his arm. "You had better go catch your flight. Amando is waiting."

Alexa turned and walked away. From a distance, Stuart saw her suddenly stop to look at him once more. She raised her right hand and flashed him the peace sign. He signed it back to her, and then watched as she disappeared into the crowd.

# 24

It was still morning and Jack was wiping down the counter in the kitchen. He had just finished cleaning the entire flat and was quite proud of his spotless work. When he heard the front door open, he dropped the rag in the sink and hurried out to meet Stuart.

Stuart stood at the door smiling. Jack could see that there was something very different about him. He had never seen Stuart look so handsome.

"It is good to be home," Stuart said, setting down his suitcase and closing the door behind him.

"I'm so glad to see you," Jack said, wanting nothing other than to just look at Stuart for a while. It took him a moment to notice the strange parcel Stuart still held under his arm.

Stuart saw Jack staring at the wrapped painting and said, "This is a gift for you." He walked towards Jack and held out the plain brown parcel.

Jack eagerly took it, then went over to the sofa and sat down. Without hesitation, he began to rip away at the paper, tossing it frivolously on the floor. Once the painting was fully revealed, he just stopped and stared. Stuart was suddenly worried. Perhaps he had made the wrong choice.

"This is absolutely bizarre!" exclaimed Jack, looking up at Stuart. He then smiled from ear to ear and said, "I love it! I don't know what it is, but there is something about this painting that makes me feel that, no matter what happens, everything in the world will be just fine."

Stuart smiled with relief. He had not been wrong. "That is exactly how I felt when I saw it," he said.

Jack looked up at Stuart. "So, I can see that you enjoyed your trip," said Jack. "You look good."

"I feel good, Jack. It was a trip like no other." Stuart then sighed as he began to consider all that was now at stake. Jack should know about the full risks before he told him anything further. He sat down on the sofa and said, "I do not want to keep any secrets from you. I never want to do that again. But you must understand that if you know the truth, you may not be safe. If I tell you everything, then you are in it as much as I, and there are no guarantees about what happens next."

Jack smiled at Stuart and said, "Five years ago, when we had our very first conversation together, I knew that there was something that connected us—something real and true. I always understood you, and I believe that you have always understood me. Despite the unfortunate things that happened in our larger lives, we could always depend on this—this one thing that kept us both grounded no matter what. I can't leave you now Stuart—not physically or emotionally. We are a part of each other, and there should never be any secrets between us. Whatever you are involved in, so am I. Can you not see in my face *the map of honor, truth, and loyalty?*"

Stuart sighed and reached for Jack's hand. He had never felt closer to him then at this very moment. "Well, I shall put the kettle on," he said. "There is a lot to explain, and I will need your help to work out a plan."

Stuart and Jack were sitting together on the sofa listening to the newest album by The Hollies. Having spent most of the day talking and planning, they now wanted only to relax and lose themselves in the music. The painting of the unicorn was hanging over the stereo, and there was a reassuring calmness within the room.

Suddenly, the sharp ring of the phone broke into the melody. The two men looked at each other. They both knew who it would be. This was just the beginning.

Stuart turned the music down, and then picked up the receiver. "Hello," he said.

"What happened in America?" demanded the Duke.

"We went to New York," replied Stuart.

"And where did you go from there?"

Stuart already had the story well worked out. "From there we went to Pennsylvania, and took a country tour. I tried to follow him as much as possible, but unfortunately, I saw nothing. He may have seemed slightly discouraged near the end of the trip, but it was unclear to me whether it was because he was old and tired, or that he had not been able to find what he was looking for. The only thing he kept saying was that he wanted to collect Pennsylvania German folk art. Perhaps that is a clue, but I saw nothing. And in the end, he did not acquire any art at all." Stuart paused, in hopes that the Duke believed him.

"And you are certain that you saw nothing else? There was nothing at all suspicious that you can recall?"

Stuart remained silent for a moment, as if he were trying to recollect. He then said, "Well, I do not know if it was significant, but there was one time when he went off in quiet conversation with an old Pennsylvania German. My own feeling was that they were not discussing anything of significance. To be honest, I have wondered if the entire trip may simply have been his way of trying to get to know me better. If that is the case, I am certain that he is very close to trusting me completely. If he does have secrets, it should not be long before I can learn them." Stuart was surprised at just how confidently he lied to the Duke.

For a while, there was only silence on the other line. Finally, the Duke said, "Tomorrow evening, you must come here and tell me exactly, day by day, everything that happened in America. I must be certain that you are not missing something. Unfortunately Stuart, you can be very simple at times. Your father had the same deficiency. It is a weakness in your blood."

"Yes of course," Stuart replied, "I shall be there tomorrow and will bring with me the daily notes that I took. Perhaps, I did overlook something." Then without another word, the Duke hung up.

Stuart put the receiver back down and turned to Jack. "We will pack our things tonight, so that we will be ready tomorrow morning when Uncle Marlon calls."

Jack took Stuart's hand in his and said, "You know that you should not worry. No matter what happens, the Duke will never win. With all my heart, I know that is the truth."

Stuart smiled. "Thank you," he said. "Thank you, for always keeping me strong. I do not know where I would be without you."

* * *

The next morning Jack made a big fry-up for them both. He wanted to be sure that they were well-fed before their journey. They had just finished their breakfast when the phone rang. Stuart picked up the receiver and said, "Hello."

"Hello Stuart. It is your Uncle Marlon. I hope that I am not disturbing you."

"No Uncle, not at all. I have just finished breakfast."

"Well, that is good then. I am phoning you because I need to confess something." Stuart was confused. He was not sure how this would fit into the plan. Marlon continued speaking. "I did not take you to America just so that we might get to know each other better. I had another motive. You see, I used you as a sort of a cover. There are people who are watching me and I needed to go to America to find some very important information. Our trip together was a ruse so that I might find what I needed to find. I now feel terrible about keeping you in the dark, and want you to understand that despite what I have done, that in no way diminishes my sincere affection for you."

Stuart felt sick. He had no idea his uncle would do this. It was clear that he was putting himself in harm's way so that Stuart would be able to escape.

"Anyway my son, I felt a great deal of guilt about the entire affair. You were so genuine in wanting to get to know your old uncle, and I truly feel that we came to understand each other very well. I hope that you do not think that I am just a sentimental old fool, but I need to tell you that I love you, my son. I'm sorry about how things have worked out. I assure you that this is for the best. I just wanted to let you know that I do love you, and also I wanted to thank you for enriching this old man's life at a time when he needed to be reminded of what really matters."

Tears began to fall down Stuart's face. "Oh Uncle Marlon," he said, "Please don't!"

"Again, I am sorry," said Marlon, "but this is for the best. Stuart, listen to me. Whenever you are facing something terrible, remember your faith in the words, *this too shall pass*. Our hearts remain true which means we are the precious children of the Kingdom of God. There is no one on earth that has the power to change that. No one on earth has the power to deny us our eternal life. No man can harm us."

"I love you, Uncle!" cried Stuart. He wanted to say more, but then there was a click, and he knew his uncle had put down the receiver.

Jack was right beside Stuart and saw how upset he was. "What's wrong?" he asked in deep concern.

"Uncle Marlon is trying to take a bullet for me," said Stuart. "I can't let him do that, Jack. I know that it may be foolish of me, but I cannot leave him alone. I have to go out there, and make sure that he is alright. I cannot just leave him in the hands of the Duke."

Jack put his hand on Stuart's shoulder. "I understand," he said. "You have to do what is in your heart, which means we will have to go with our plan B."

Stuart put his hand on Jack's. "You know that this may not be a happy ending for us. It may just be like one of those sad movies you love so much. Are you prepared for that?"

Jack looked at Stuart and in his best acting voice said, "Alas Sir Robin, *our doubts are traitors, and make us lose the good we oft might win by fearing to attempt.*"

Stuart smiled at Jack's courageous words. "Then, let us do that which we need to do," he said as he kissed Jack goodbye, and then quickly headed out the door. There was no time to lose.

# 25

Stuart pulled up to the cottage. The front door was left wide open. He knew that this was a bad sign.

Before he had even entered, he could see that everything had been torn apart. Furniture was overturned and upholstery was ripped into pieces. Drawers lay on the floor, their contents spilled everywhere. Someone had searched every inch of the cottage.

"Uncle," called Stuart, still trying to hold out hope. There was no answer.

Stuart stepped over many broken objects as he made his way towards the kitchen. When he was in sight of the open door, he could see that his uncle was lying on the floor. Marlon was on an angle, and only his legs could be seen from the living room. "Uncle!" Stuart called as he dashed into the kitchen. He then stood frozen in disbelief at what he saw. Nothing could have prepared him for this! Uncle Marlon's body was lying lifeless in a pool of blood. His head was missing.

Stuart quickly turned away. He began to wail in anger and grief. He pounded his fist upon the kitchen counter and screamed, "You evil son of a bitch!" For a few moments, he just tried to breathe deeply and regain control.

Picking up a white tablecloth that had been pulled out of a drawer, he carefully covered his uncle's body. He then sat down on the floor next to him and held his uncle's hand. "Oh Uncle Marlon, I promise you this. He will not win! No matter what it takes, I will defeat him!"

Stuart wept for a little while longer, before pulling himself up off the floor. He did not want to just leave his uncle's body like that, but there were things to be done. Time was important, and he had to move on. Stuart took in a deep breath, and made his way out to his car. Driving to the end of the lane, he turned the wheel south towards Weymouth.

* * *

Jack had not heard from Stuart for several hours and was very worried. When the phone finally did ring, he jumped up and grabbed the receiver. "Stuart?" he asked anxiously.

"Oh Jack," cried Stuart, at first barely able to get the words out, "he's been murdered!"

Jack felt Stuart's pain as if it were his own. "Oh no! I'm so sorry, Stuart." For a moment, he almost forgot what this phone call meant for him.

"They took his head, Jack!" exclaimed Stuart, who was filling with rage. "They cut off Uncle Marlon's head! What kind of a filthy animal takes another man's head? The Duke is not even a human being! He's worth even less than a dog!" Stuart wanted to make sure the Duke heard every word.

Jack knew what was coming next, and was prepared to do what was needed.

"I have to tell you something important, Jack," said Stuart. "But before I do, I just need you to forgive me for everything I have ever done to hurt you."

Jack was surprised. He realized that this was not part of the plan. This was something Stuart wanted to say—just in case.

"In the past, I know I have been unfair to you. You tried to help me, but I did not listen. Will you please forgive me for the many times I hurt you?"

Tears began to well-up in Jack's eyes. Did this mean he may never see Stuart again? "I have always forgiven you, Stuart. I have never doubted what was in your heart."

For a moment, there was only silence on the other end of the phone and then Stuart said,

"I now need to tell you that the documents I told you about—the ones that Uncle Marlon said he had—well, I took those documents. And because the old goat did not find them at the cottage, he will certainly be coming after me next. I hid them in the flat, Jack. Please do not look at them, as it is best that you not know what is contained there. What I need is for you to keep them safe, until I can return. I don't know when that will be, but it may be a while. In the meantime, the documents are hidden inside of the large porcelain unicorn. The first one you ever gave to me. Do you understand?"

"Yes," replied Jack, trying to hold back the sobs. "I understand perfectly."

"And before I go, there's just one more thing."

Jack waited, wondering what it could be. Then he heard Stuart say, "No matter the outcome. Remember Hamlet's words, *There's a divinity that shapes our ends. Rough-hew them how we will.*" After that, Stuart was gone.

* * *

Stuart hung up the receiver and then rested his forehead against the payphone. "God, please keep Jack safe," he whispered. He turned and opened the phone booth door. As he walked back to his car, he looked around the deserted warehouse district. A single white truck pulled out of from a loading dock close to where he was parked, but other than that, there was no sign of human life. Even though he knew the lively port where he was headed was only a short drive from this place, at that moment, it seemed as if he were the only person now left in the entire world.

He opened the car door and got in. His plan was risky and he knew it, but he had to be sure those papers reached Scotland. As he sat in his car, he thought for a moment about Marlon, and all that he had said on the trip to America. He knew that his uncle was not afraid to die. Marlon believed completely in The Kingdom of God. Stuart wondered how he was to keep believing like his uncle, in the face of such intense grief. *This too shall pass*, he thought to himself.

172

Just at that moment, he found himself remembering the face of the little girl on the bridge. He suddenly could feel her presence, and that feeling of amazing peace was beginning to return. All of his crippling anger and pain was slowly vanishing. *"If I believe, I will see the glory of God,"* he whispered. He then looked up through his windshield and saw the clear blue sky above. It was a beautiful day and several white seagulls glided over the wind. Stuart could not only see, but he could also feel how free and alive they were. It was as if he were flying alongside of them. For a few seconds longer, he remained only in that peaceful stillness. Finally breaking the silence, he began to pray. *Oh God, You have freed me from my fear. Wherever You want me to go, then I will go. I am Yours completely, and I surrender to Your Will.*

Stuart took in a deep breath. There was now no doubt in his mind that Uncle Marlon was right. They would live forever. No matter what could be done to his body, no one on earth could touch his soul. He smiled and then turned the key in the ignition. There was a loud thunderous boom and a bright flash of light. In an instant, Stuart had ascended in a ball of fire.

# 26

Jack was ready for them when they busted through the flat door. He looked surprised, and shouted, "Who are you! What do you want?" There were two large young men in suits and an older man who Jack knew must be the Duke. One of the two large men moved near Jack, preparing to restrain him if it might become necessary.

The Duke looked at Jack and sneered. "You are Jack?" He looked him up and down. "A fat low-bred faggot like yourself must know some fine tricks to land a man like our Stuart."

The insult did not bother Jack. He had heard worse. But what he did not like was the way the Duke referred to Stuart as "our Stuart." Still, he just kept silent for now. He had to play it right.

The Duke looked around the room and saw the table with all of Stuart's unicorns. He went over and picked up the large porcelain one.

Jack made a lunge towards him, but the henchman quickly moved behind him, grabbed his arms and held him in place. "Leave that alone!" he yelled.

The Duke just glared at him, and tipped the unicorn upside down. He could see that something was tucked inside of the opening at the bottom. He then held it up and casually dropped it to the floor. The unicorn shattered into pieces revealing a brown envelope hidden within. "Now what is this?" said the Duke, grinning from ear to ear. He reached down and picked up the envelope. It did not seem as heavy as it should be. He quickly tore it open and out fell a single playing card—the joker.

The Duke's face was beginning to turn red with anger. He marched up to Jack, who was still being restrained, and put his hand to Jack's throat. "Where is the information," he hissed through his clenched teeth.

Jack smiled. "It is now on a boat headed for somewhere far away from England," he replied.

The Duke was confused. "What do you mean?" he asked, as he released Jack's throat.

Jack smiled triumphantly at the Duke. "Stuart sent you on a wild goose chase. The documents were never hidden here. Stuart always had the envelope. He tricked you into coming here so that he could get the documents safely away."

Jack could see that the Duke was becoming more enraged. He turned to one of his men and screamed, "Bloody hell!" The man did not know how to respond, and only looked submissively down.

The Duke then turned back to Jack. "Are you lying? You are truly telling me that the documents were with Stuart?"

Suddenly, Jack realized that something was wrong. Something had happened to Stuart. "What did you do?" he demanded, even though he was afraid to hear the answer.

The Duke waved the henchman off of Jack. "Oh let him go," he said. "There is no point in going any further. It is over."

It was not quite over for Jack. He rushed towards the Duke and again demanded, "What has happened to Stuart?"

The Duke was upset, thinking about the valuable documents that were lost. Without giving it much thought, he casually answered, "When that bloody car blew up, so did those papers."

Jack felt his knees crumble beneath him, and he was on the floor. "Oh no," he cried. "Oh Stuart!"

The Duke looked at Jack with disgust. He had just lost the most important thing he could ever possess, and now this crying faggot was annoying him. "Come," he said to his two men. "There is no reason to remain here any longer."

Suddenly, before anyone could stop him, Jack leapt to his feet. With one solid blow, he smashed his fist straight into the Duke's face. The Duke immediately fell backwards onto the floor. His head hit hard against the wood. One of the henchmen was on Jack in an instant. The other knelt beside the Duke who, at first, was not moving at all. Eventually, the Duke showed signs of life when he coughed on some blood in his throat. His hired man helped him to sit up, and bright red blood began to drip from his nose and onto his chest. It stained black into his dark grey silk shirt.

At first, the Duke could not think or see straight. He tried to focus on the man who knelt beside him, but could not understand what was happening. He then looked around the room. That was when he saw the painting on the wall. The great white unicorn appeared so powerful, alive and triumphant, and the dead empty eyes of the ape stared straight out at him. The Duke found himself shuddering in fear.

"Your Grace, are you alright?" asked the henchman.

The Duke did not respond. He could not take his eyes from the painting.

"Are you alright?" the man asked again, this time louder.

His words finally seemed to get through when the Duke absently replied, "I…I do not know." He was still unable to look away from the painting.

"Should I kill him?" asked the other man, who was holding Jack.

The Duke finally forced his gaze from the picture on the wall and tried to focus only on the floorboards. He continued to feel disoriented and confused. It was then that he realized his man was now holding a white handkerchief to his bleeding nose. The white cloth was quickly turning to red.

Again the man asked, "Should I kill him, Your Grace."

The Duke wanted to scream 'yes, kill him now!' but his head was hurting, and the image of the painting kept clouding his mind with frightening thoughts. Before he knew it, he found himself meekly murmuring, "No."

The two men looked at each other, and then grabbed the Duke by his two arms. They slowly helped him to his feet. The

Duke looked old and broken between them. Without even looking at Jack, they then silently left the flat, closing the door behind them.

Jack was exhausted and still in shock. The silence in the room was beginning to crush him, and all he could think was that he needed to fill it with music. Jack went over to the stereo and put on his favorite Hollies album. He then sat on the sofa, as the first song began to play. Tears were streaming down his face as he thought about Stuart. They had talked about this possibility, but talking couldn't really prepare for the reality of it. Jack looked at the broken pieces of the unicorn on the floor. Part of him wondered how he could possibly go on alone, but he knew that he had to. He had to for Stuart. *"There is special providence in the fall of a sparrow,"* he whispered to himself.

# 27

Jack walked down the old broken cobblestone road with a suitcase in one hand and a large rectangular parcel under the other arm. Small dowdy row houses lined both sides of the street, and children seemed to be everywhere. They ran up and down, laughing and playing in natural defiance of the bleakness that surrounded them. Jack smiled as he remembered what that was like to be a child. It was a condition where joy and fun managed to blossom despite the harshest of conditions. *Perhaps that is why Jesus taught that you have to be like a child to be able to enter The Kingdom of God*, he thought to himself.

Jack stopped at the old green painted door. It had been this same color forever. He knocked and then waited.

The door opened, and Jack stepped in, dropping his suitcase on the floor. He then fell into the arms of his mother. His sorrow poured out, and he began to weep like a little boy. "Oh Mum!" he cried. "I wish you could have met him."

His mother held him with one arm and closed the door with the other. "It's alright, love. It'll be alright," she said soothingly.

Jack's mother took him by his hand and led him over to a chair. She caringly sat him down at the table. Stroking his hair, she softly said, "Let me put the kettle on. We could both use a brew." Stepping over to the nearby kitchen counter, she began to fill the kettle with water.

Jack put the rectangular package on the table. He brushed his fingers over the surface, and sighed.

"What's that?" asked his mother.

"This," said Jack, still trying to hold back the tears, "is the last gift Stuart ever gave me. Would you like to see it?"

"Yes, of course I would," replied his mother, who sat down at the table and smiled warmly at him.

Jack tore off the brown paper and showed her the painting. "Oh!" she said, trying to think of something nice to say. "It's—it's very different—very modern indeed. But I'm afraid I don't know too much about art."

Jack laughed at his mother's reaction. He hadn't laughed since he had last laughed with Stuart. It felt good to know that it was still possible. "It's a bit of an inside joke," he tried to explain.

Jack's mother patted his hand and said, "Well, if it's important to you, then it's important to me. And you can hang it anywhere you like. It may scare old Mrs. Rafferty when she comes over for a cuppa, but she stays too long anyway. That woman doesn't know when to belt-up." Jack smiled as he knew that this was no exaggeration.

Jack looked into his mother's eyes and said, "Mum, there is something more about this painting—something very important."

His mother stared at the painting again, and then looked questioningly at Jack. Before she could ask, Jack turned the painting over and began to tear off the felt backing. Inside of the canvas was a large plain brown envelope. Jack pulled it out and smiled proudly.

"Now what is that, love?" asked his mother in wonderment.

"This, Mum, is what Stuart gave his life for. Inside of this envelope is very important information. It is so important that it just may help save the world one day," answered Jack.

His mother did not know what to say. She looked in amazement at Jack. His eyes were sparkling in a way she had never seen before. Feeling very proud of her son, she then stared in awe at the plain brown envelope he held in his hand.

"How do you fancy a trip to Scotland?" Jack asked.

His mother smiled from ear to ear. "Oh, you know that I have always wanted to go to Scotland!" she happily exclaimed.

"Well then Mummy," he said in the best upper society accent he could muster, "let us have our tea, and then I shall help you pack. As of this moment, we are now secret agents on a secret mission to save the world." Jack triumphantly waved the envelope in the air.

Jack's mother lovingly placed her hands on either side of her son's face and kissed his forehead. Her favorite television show was *The Saint* and the idea of becoming a spy had been her long-time secret fantasy. "Oh Jack!" she said, "You know I'm up for it!"

"I knew I could count on you, Mum. Together, we will make the best spies this world has ever seen," he said.

"No one could be better than us," replied his mother. "But before we go anywhere, I'll caution you on one very important thing and one thing only."

"And what is that?" Jack asked.

She looked at him very seriously and replied, "If it happens that we meet up with *Simon Templar*, then you must understand that he is all mine."

"Oh Mum!" Jack said as he burst out laughing. It was then that he was sure he heard Stuart laugh too.

Rose sat on Mrs. Benson's front step happily eating a chocolate ice cream cone. She looked down at Julia who sat beside her and said, "Sorry, but you know you can't have any. You just get it stuck all over you face." Julia only looked straight ahead with her pretty brown eyes, and smiled contentedly.

This was the first Saturday Jeannie was to clean Mrs. Benson's house. It had taken her a while to find a new job to fill the one she had lost at the church. This one was in the nearby city, so it was a little farther from home. However, she was able to take it because there was a bus that went almost straight to the front door. Mrs. Benson appeared to be a kind and fair employer, and did not mind Jeannie bringing her daughter along. It was a pleasant surprise when Mrs. Benson had even been so nice as to offer Rose an ice-cream cone on a hot day.

Rose quickly finished off the last of the ice-cream. She then picked up Julia and walked out to the street. She looked up one way and then the other. There was nothing much to see, just houses and trees. She then looked back at Mrs. Benson's house. It was a large old brick home with some windows in the attic. Rose looked all the way up to the top of the roof and was surprised see a stone tower rising up behind it. "Look Julia," she said. "There's a secret castle."

Rose wanted to see the castle up close. She walked down past three houses and around the corner. She followed a wooden fence until she came to the place where the tower would be. There it was, reaching far up into the sky! At the bottom was an arched doorway, and the sign on the front lawn said,

*St. Mary Magdalene*
*Catholic Church*

Rose could read that it was a church, but she still wanted to pretend it was a castle. "Let's take a closer look Julia, but be careful of fire breathing dragons.

She walked up the big stone steps to the large wooden door. It was wide open. Rose peeked inside, but there was no one to be seen. She slipped in and just stood at the back waiting to see if someone would come and chase her out. No one appeared.

She looked over at a table full of lit candles. It was very pretty, but she wondered why no one had made a wish and blown them out. It seemed like a big waste of wishes.

Rose did not want to walk up the middle of the church where someone might see her. Instead, she moved slowly up the side, past the long rows of pews. This church must have many more people than her old one. She looked at the amazing high arches, the large colorful windows and the gold that seemed to be everywhere. This certainly seemed more like a castle than a church.

As she reached the front of the church, she moved to the center to get a closer look at the altar. "A very rich king must own this place," she said to Julia.

To one side of the altar was a statue of a blonde woman in long blue and white robe. She had pink cheeks, and red lips like she had just been at beauty parlor with Lizzy's mother. Rose then looked up high above the Altar. She stood frozen in shock! She had never seen anything like this before!

There in dim light of the church was Jesus nailed on the cross. He was pale as death and there was red blood dripping everywhere. His face was sad and broken and his body looked starved. He wore only a rag around his middle.

Rose could feel herself begin to cry. Those church people had lied again! They said that Jesus had been taken down, but he hadn't! He was still there suffering on the cross! Why do they lie so much?

"I'm sorry Jesus," she whispered up to him. "They told me they let you down, but they didn't, did they? They left you up there; just so people can come and get scared, and gawk at you. I'm sorry they did this. I didn't know about it because they lied to me."

Rose wanted to do something to make it all right. She just couldn't stand to see Jesus suffer like this. But what could she do? She was just a little girl and little girls have no power in this world. Then Rose suddenly remembered the falling star and how she had not used her wish. She still had her falling star wish! She had not thrown it away on something foolish. This was a powerful wish—a wish that came straight from heaven.

Rose looked up at Jesus' sad broken face. She set Julia down on the altar, and put her palms together in prayer. "Jesus, I love you. I don't want you to be up there anymore. But today, I'm just a little girl, who can't do much. Right now, all I have is a wish, but the good news is that it is a falling star wish. Falling star wishes are powerful and always come true.  So I am going to give it to you. Here is my wish:

*I wish that someday I will be big and strong enough to do anything, and then I will come back here. I will take those thorns off your head. I will take those nails out of your feet. I will take those nails out of your hands. Then you can come down on the ground again. We can get you some bandages, and then I will help you find what they did with your clothes. You will be free again! You can walk around like you did before, and tell stories, and love people, and make people do good things again. This is my one-and-only-most-powerful falling star wish. I promise you Jesus, that I will be back, and I will make everything alright again.*

*Amen."*

www.ingramcontent.com/pod-product-compliance
Lightning Source LLC
Chambersburg PA
CBHW070031120726
47909CB00003B/1126